Blood and Beauty
and Other Weird Tales
Jeff Chapman

Blood and Beauty and Other Weird Tales
Jeff Chapman

The stories contained within this eBook are works of fiction. All material is either the product of the author's imagination or is used in a fictitious manner. Any resemblance to actual persons (living or dead) or to actual events is entirely coincidental.

Cover: *Pan and Psyche* by Sir Edward Burne-Jones (1833 - 1898).

Contents

Good King David
Hamlet meets Absalom in Biblical fantasy

About the Author
Publication History
*This story contains adult material.

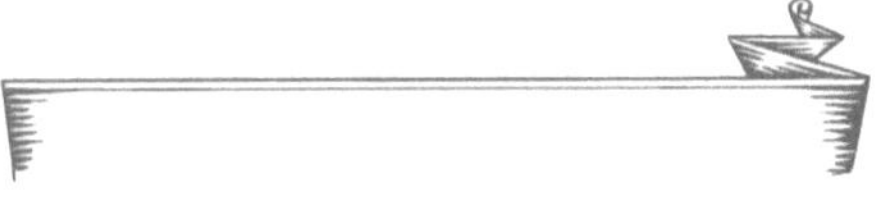

Blood and Beauty

He scented the father and the six daughters before he heard them. Every new moon they danced, skipping through the heather, leaping and spinning. Their hair waved in the breeze, golden at the scalp before darkening to green along its length.

The monstrosity crouched lower into the blackberry brambles. Gray hair grew in wavy strands around his loins and legs, which ended in cloven hooves. His torso and arms suggested a man but wiry, yellow hair veiled his white skin in a jaundiced halo. A black mane ringed his face. Deep-seated yellow eyes peered over a broad, flat nose, and from the tip of his nostrils through his upper lip sliced a cleft from which his tongue shot to taste the air. Retractable claws adorned his fingers.

Ignoring the tantalizing berries, the half lion, half satyr risked inching forward to admire Feena, his lust and love. If they saw him, the dryads would vanish into the forest, driven off by his ugliness.

He watched for hours, yearning to hold her, to touch her tender skin. Twice she danced within reach. A single bound and she would have known the strength of his grasp, suffered his lips and tongue, but Salton checked his desire: he wanted her love.

When the dryads left the clearing, Salton rolled onto his back, waiting for limberness to return to his aching knees. *He must have her.* The old father dryad would suffer, but surely he wouldn't sacrifice them all to keep one.

Their magical hearts beat deep in the forest in a grove all but inaccessible to the woodsman's ax. Salton journeyed daily from his cave to caress Feena's tree, to lick and sniff her sap, and to offer his devotion. Each hemlock grew perfectly straight with delicate branches fanning out from its bole. The new growth emerged dark yellow as if the branches were tipped with gold.

The father's tree stood in the center beside a blackened, limbless trunk, which marked the mother's grave where lightning had done its worst. She must have screamed as she burned alive. Salton thanked the gods he had not heard it.

The father recoiled as Salton approached, creaking and bending as if the satyr-lion brought forth a mighty wind. Salton touched the father's bole and pressed his fingers into the furrowed bark. "Is my ugliness a threat, Lerhem? I had no part in how nature made me. Let me love your daughter."

Lerhem did not speak. The dryads, the squirrels, and even the birds fell dumb with anticipation.

"Your silence insults me." His cleft parted as he snarled through jagged teeth ḻend red gums. "You condemn me for nature's abuse, but I *am* master of what I do."

Claws shot from his fingers and he dragged the points through the furrows, cutting to the tree's flesh. Lerhem screeched and his branches shook.

Salton withdrew his hand. His claws folded into his fingertips. "I can hurt you in ways unimaginable."

Delicate whisperings flitted among the trees like butterflies. Then the chatter ceased and a deep voice resounded in his head.

"Such a union would be unnatural. It is forbidden."

Salton roared at the sky, baring his cat fangs from point to root. The hemlocks quivered, as with the first gusts from a storm.

He raised his claws and looked about the circle at so much beauty and perfection. How could an honest plea for love be forbidden? His hand snapped downward, leaving a five-fingered gash across Lerhem's trunk.

"DID YOU HEAR THAT?" asked the elder of the two woodsmen. The handle of his ax rested on his shoulder and graying hair poked below the edge of his red, wool cap.

"It's too far. We shouldn't be going this way." Like his father, the son carried an ax and wore a red cap, but his black hair curled up below the neck, and a thick coil of rope hung from his shoulder.

The older man stopped. They were following a deer trail and something else through a stretch of unexplored forest. The noonday sun stabbed at the broad-leaf canopy overhead, pressing the forest to yield from the black of night to the cloudy gray of twilight. Squirrels scurried among the oaks. A woodpecker's knock reverberated. A grunt told them of feral pigs feasting on nuts. All these sounds were familiar and unnoticed except when they chose to listen.

"These woods are strange, Father. I can feel something here."

"Aye. Perhaps we should go back. But look at these oaks. No one has ever cut here."

They craned their necks to see the treetops well over a hundred feet above them.

"Too big for us," said the son. He pointed at the base of a massive bole. "Would take five men, maybe even six or seven, just to circle that."

Three delicate notes from a flute fluttered past.

"That," said the father.

The son shook his head. "What is it?"

The father broke through the undergrowth toward the source, drawn like a wolf to blood. The son followed, his senses clouded and dim. He felt drunk, not the way of the mead he drank to excess with his friends, but on enchantment. A witch might live out here or faeries, coaxing them to a cauldron or an Eden of no return.

For hours they traveled in fits and starts, leaving the oak and walnut forest for hemlock and pine, resolving to turn back only to plunge ahead again when the flute whispered. They emerged from the forest into a grove of golden hemlocks, which grew in a ring around another hemlock and a denuded bole, gray and cracked from the weather.

They gaped at the perfectly proportioned trees, at the green boughs tipped with gold, a species living only in myth.

"It can't be," said the son. "It's an illusion. We're bewitched."

"A gift," answered the father. "We were meant to find these." He stepped toward the fairest tree, grasped the lowest branch and broke off the tip with its mixture of green and golden needles. "Is this an illusion?"

The satyr-lion hiding in the shadows winced as his beloved shrieked. Already the unanticipated had soiled Salton's scheme. Though these woodsmen could not hear it, the trees screeched and screamed like horses in a burning stable.

With one hand Salton pressed the halves of his cleft lip together and with the other brought the hollow reeds bound with grass to his mouth. The notes diverted the woodsmen.

"And this is the grandest of them all," said the father, approaching Lerhem. "Go on, see if you can reach around it."

The son embraced the trunk but his fingers did not touch.

"At least six more hands," said the father. "We must keep this place secret."

"Who would believe? It will take us a week to drag these home through the woods." Startled, he pointed to five parallel gouges in the bark.

"A lion, possibly. Marking his territory," said the father.

"It's too dangerous here."

"The woods are always dangerous and so is a prize worthy of song and story. We should cut one now."

The son pointed at Feena. "The fairest and the lightest."

Salton sucked in a breath. His lips quivered and his fingers shook as the two men approached Feena. The dryads squealed like dying rabbits, piercing his eardrums and shattering his concentration, which he needed most for the spell.

He squeezed his eyes shut, focusing on the words, on the two men who must forget. He repeated the words, catching their rhythm, for if that rhythm was imperfect, the spell would fail. Notes shot from the flute toward the men, who stopped before landing their blow.

They looked at one another, searching for a glimmer of comprehension, a landmark in a fog bank, but found nothing. Where? Why? What? The questions rolled about in their minds, sloshing to and fro, and in unison they shouldered their axes and strode from the grove, following the obscure path that had led them there.

THE BOY CROUCHED LOWER behind a fallen log and fountain of ferns as his father and older brother marched past, staring ahead, not speaking or singing, not smiling or frowning. Their sharp eyes did not scan the forest at all: most unusual and dangerous.

He looked back to the golden hemlocks, then slunk along the trail until he was out of sight and hearing. A giant boar crossed their path, grunted, and shook his tusks. But the men marched toward it, and if the boar had not charged away, they would have fallen over the beast's bristled back. They suffered an enchantment. About this, the boy harbored no doubts.

As the father's grip loosened, the branch that he had broken from one of the hemlocks fell out of his hand. The boy picked it up, not fully believing what he had seen until he felt the prick of the green and golden needles in his palm. He dropped the branch in a satchel, where it joined the berries he had been gathering.

The spell wore off as the pair reached familiar woods and the men began wondering at the passage of the day without cutting any trees.

The boy caught up to them. "No luck today, Father?"

The men exchanged a troubled glance. "We didn't find a tree worthy to cut today, Doran." He slapped his youngest son's shoulder. "I hope your berry picking was more profitable."

"Not so much," said Doran. "But I did find a worthy tree. I found a golden hemlock."

His older brother laughed. "And I saw a centaur mounting a river nymph."

"You saw a dying pine," said the father. "You're as likely to see a golden hemlock as a satyr."

The two men laughed as they turned toward the cottage.

Doran pulled the branch from his satchel. "Is this a dying pine?"

SALTON BRUSHED THE rounded nubs of his claws across Feena's trunk. The wiry hair growing on his hands and fingers caught in the bark, but he took no notice. He hummed a ballad, stroking Feena in time with the music, as if Feena was a violin and Salton the bow. The dryad giggled from the tickling.

"I would never let them hurt you," he whispered.

"No, you would not. But could you stop them?"

Salton growled deep in his throat. "You underestimate me. I would have torn their limbs and sliced their throats and drenched your roots in their blood had they struck you."

"And if they had chopped at my father or sisters?"

"They didn't. They chose the most perfect."

"If you are to have me then you must speak plainly."

"Then tell *me* plainly," said Salton. "Will you have me?"

"Do my father and I have a choice between life and death?"

"It was your father who refused me. To be ugly is to be cursed in his eyes. But do you blame me for seeking a lover's bliss?"

"I've reproached you for what you did. Not why you did it. My father is calling you."

Salton pressed his cheek against Feena and shot his tongue through his cleft to catch a drop of sap. "It won't be long, my love."

"I cannot leave without my father's permission," said Feena.

But Salton did not answer. He well knew this and growled as he approached Lerhem.

"You play reckless games," said Lerhem. "For centuries we stood here undisturbed until an abomination showed death the way."

Salton shrieked, his cry echoing through the woods and valleys as he slashed Lerhem. Amber rivulets sprang from the gouges. "Give me Feena and I'll protect you. I'll stand between all of you and any threat."

"A harbinger of danger as our savior? Your promises offer no comfort."

The grove shivered with whisperings, urgent and plaintive. Salton struggled to pick out the individual voices, to determine their tone, whether for or against him.

Lerhem groaned. "You have imperiled us, who are rooted to the earth, the victims and beneficiaries of happenstance. I do not trust your spells, but since you value your desires above our eternal destruction, we must accept your protection. I expect nothing fruitful from this union. Let us never speak of it again."

SALTON GATHERED REEDS growing in the shallows of a lake and wove them into a pallet which he laid over dried moss. Across the pallet he sprinkled flower petals from every orchid he could find. His wedding bed complete, he hunted a stag, creeping up on the foraging animal at the edge of a meadow. He sprang onto the beast's back, sinking his claws into its flank and chest before crushing its windpipe between his jaws. He savored the blood dripping from his mane and hands, blood lust driving him to eat his fill, consume it raw, but for his bride he resisted.

He roasted the deer on a spit at the mouth of his cave until the meat glistened and bubbled with melting fat.

His preparations consumed a day and a night and though Lerhem and his daughters feared the time when the sun crossed the sky, Salton went to collect his bride just as the sun rose behind the eastern peaks.

"Will you hide among the hawthorn to set an ambush or wait in the open to frighten any comers without a fight?" said Lerhem.

"Today, I take my bride home." Salton stroked Feena's cheek. "Strategy is tomorrow. You've made me wait long enough."

"You brought them here," said Lerhem. "You've given away our secrets."

Salton took Feena's hand and led her from the grove, from Lerhem's blustering, from the whispering trees.

"Father and my sisters are very frightened by what you did when you brought the woodsmen. We should not leave them during the day."

"The woodsmen have forgotten everything, and I've prepared a feast and a bed of flowers for you."

Salton talked as they trod the forest, recounting his hunt for orchids and the slaying of the stag. He bade her to sit on a log in the cool shadow of his cave's entrance. He tore meat from the roasting deer and poured wine in wooden cups. Feena nibbled at the meat, respecting Salton's kindness. The wine she gulped and after the third cup Salton moved the flask within her reach.

He ate his fill, swallowing chunks of meat whole and snapping bones to suck the marrow. Grease and wine clotted his mane. He recounted the many nights he'd watched her dance. Feena listened and smiled and when his confidence overflowed, he risked a question.

"Do you find me repulsive?"

"You're a creature with talents, like any other. Your music is certainly not repulsive."

"Ah, my flute. Many days my only companion." He wiped his greasy fingers on the goat hair covering his thighs, then raised the hollowed reeds to his lips before turning his back so she would not see him holding his cleft together.

He played a lively tune, tapping a hoof with the rhythm, and Feena danced around the ashen coals that smoked beneath the stag's carcass. His flute bore magic and any song had the power to bewitch a mortal, but Salton had no magic to bewitch a dryad.

"Why do you turn your back?" she asked.

"I am shy."

"You needn't be." Feena leapt and pranced about the coals to a song in her head. "Why would I laugh at such sweet sounds. You must play for my father and sisters when we dance in the clearing."

"I want nothing more."

"I'll speak to Father. He'll think differently when he hears you play."

Salton laid down his flute. "Could you love a face like mine?"

"I could love the man behind it, if he no longer threatened my family."

"There was no other way."

"You didn't try. You could have befriended us, entertained us with your music. Other satyrs have done so."

"Perhaps I acted rashly, but your father is stubborn."

"Cautious. As he must be. He cares only for my welfare."

"As do I. Come see the bed I've prepared before the flower petals lose their fragrance."

He took her hand and led her into his cave. His hooves clicked against the stone floor. He lit two torches, whose light revealed the pallet covered with flowers. Feena crouched to admire his work. Her beauty glowed in the wavering, yellow light. Salton stood in silhouette, his ugliness for a moment blotted out.

Feena stretched out atop the flower petals, which curled around her shoulders and hips like water. She rolled her head, taking in the myriad scents and then beckoned Salton to join her. He caressed her and bathed her with his lips, repeating "I love you" after each kiss. He could hold back no longer and mounted her, fulfilling his longings of many years. He thrust gently, taking her virginity, and as they moved together, she writhed beneath him and moaned with what Salton assumed to be passion.

Her cries multiplied. Her movements became erratic. Her fingers dug into Salton's shoulder blades. Equating her response to his prowess, he redoubled the fury of his lovemaking, his hooves clacking against the floor in time with his thrusts. Feena cried a long, diminishing scream, and then her arms went lax, sliding off Salton's shoulders. Her eyes rolled back as white as snow, and she vanished, leaving Salton to thrash about in the pool of flower petals, unfulfilled and alone.

He leapt to his hooves, cursing whatever magic Lerhem had used to summon his daughter and defile their agreement. He grabbed his flute and ran toward the hemlock grove, shouting curses. "I'll strip all the bark from his bole," he swore, "and set a fire at its base."

Dusk fell as he ascended the knoll to the grove, hoarse from running and shouting. The sun burned red to the west above the treetops. Salton stopped. The fading light flooded the grove unfiltered. Seven stumps, their tops hewn roughly with axes, sweeping to points and ridges like snow-covered mountains, marked what had once been. Sticky rivers of sap oozed from the wounds and trailed to the ground where woodchips lay scattered around each stump. Gold and green needles littered the ground, the hallowed ground of Salton's love.

The great trees lay where they had fallen, all pointing east as was the woodsmen's custom, some paean to the gods that Salton did not understand. He stumbled among the remains and counted six logs. The woodsmen had shorn the branches from two of them.

He knelt beside Feena's stump. They had taken her. He roared, wrapping his arms and legs around her decapitated trunk, and mixed his tears with her sap until the sap liquefied and Salton's tears and Feena's blood ran together.

He rose when the moon shone overhead, its gray light touching upon the hallowed ground for the first time in centuries. The grove was silent and empty. Feena's words echoed in his head. *You brought the woodsmen. We shouldn't leave them alone.* But he had seen the woodsmen work before. Tomorrow, they would bring horses and more men.

He followed the trail left by Feena's log, where the woodsmen had dragged it through the forest. The trail reeked of Feena. When he stepped from the woods into the garden behind the woodsmen's cottage, a pair of dogs barked, but Salton silenced them with a few notes from his flute.

Stepping over the sleeping dogs, he searched the yard but Feena's bole was gone, too valuable perhaps to leave unsecured.

Following her scent brought him to the woodpile where her smaller branches had been stacked to cure with the other firewood, pieces of his beloved reduced to kindling, fuel for the family's cook fires.

He knelt before Feena's remains, took up his flute and played a tune in a minor key that leapt and fell with a building frenzy. At first his body tingled, then it ached, then his blood burned through every vein, a poison to him and any creature.

With the last of his failing strength, he gashed his neck with his claws before collapsing across the stack of Feena's branches. His blood boiled out of his neck and soaked the wood with toxins. The satyr's body diminished and evaporated. Salton's flute lay where he had dropped it, beside the woodpile and free of blood.

"DORAN. DORAN," CALLED his father from outside. His mother nodded, so Doran left his porridge to attend his father.

"Old Mrs. Cowper wants two bundles of wood. Take a satchel. She'll have seven onions for you."

He nodded and hurried inside to fetch a bag. An errand meant a trip through the village, a chance for something out of the ordinary to happen. His mother bade him to count the onions, and as he passed through the doorway, he met his older brother carrying firewood.

"The new hemlock," said the eldest brother to his mother. "Father says it's ready. That it'll burn sweet and hot."

"What?" said Doran. "I should be here when it burns."

"There's plenty of it to burn, little brother. We have all winter."

"Your brother's right," said his mother. "Now you have a reason not to tarry."

Doran frowned. Arguing would get him nowhere. He stomped outside where he tied the bundles of firewood and slung them over his back. He took off for the village, resentment driving his legs to a trot. He had led them to the hemlock grove. He should be the first to smell the wood burn.

Inside his tunic, the flute he had found beside the woodpile months before thumped against his chest with each stride. At least he had held the gold coins that the man at the mill had given his father for the logs. His father said they were now a rich family.

His trot slowed to a walk. He greeted the neighbors he passed but to their surprise did not stop to talk. The old woman Cowper put seven onions in his satchel, one at a time with a trembling hand. He set off for home, intending to follow the road and brook no distractions, but a sweet, young voice at a turn in the lane stopped him.

Amilee, the blacksmith's daughter, beckoned to him from a stand of birches. Doran left the path for the trees. What was some smoking wood to Amilee's bosom and lips? He had kissed her once, a hurried peck, but the memory had lingered for days. Her family guarded her virtue like a king his crown jewels. The father had ambitions for her marriage and a woodsman's son did not figure into them.

But maybe, Doran thought, with the wealth of the hemlocks, his prospects had risen.

"Why haven't you come to see me," Amilee said, "to tell me all about the hemlocks?"

"You know why I don't come to see you." They threaded their way deeper among the birches. As always, she teased him without mercy.

"You should ask my father to be an apprentice."

"And sweat over a hot fire all day?"

"And see me every day."

"Apprentices aren't rich, Amilee, but a finder of golden hemlocks is."

"Will you find more? I would love to see one."

"I don't know. I might have a knack for it, so maybe."

Doran sat beneath two birches whose boles joined at the ground. Purple and yellow wildflowers stared at the sun amid the grass cropped short by flocks of sheep on the common pasture. Amilee tucked her skirt under her legs as she joined him. Her black hair was braided into plaits tied behind her head. As an unmarried woman, she did not cover her hair.

"How did you find them?" she asked.

"It's a secret."

"Even from me?"

Doran touched the flute as he scratched his chest. "Listen to this. I've been practicing." Notes tumbled from the flute as Doran blew into the reeds and some coalesced into a melody.

Amilee giggled. "You plan to be a bard now?"

Doran ignored her. Amilee swayed, weaving to the current of the song; her eyes narrowed and her lips pursed. Doran played more as the music inspired him and Amilee seemed to enjoy it. She scooted closer, pressed her bosom against his arm and crossed her legs over his. The heat of her breath inflamed his cheeks like the bellows in her father's forge.

He stared at the tops of her breasts exposed above her bodice and followed their curves to the crease in between. So close he could touch them with the slightest move of his hand from the flute. Her softness stirred his heart to beat in rhythm with his playing.

Amilee knocked the flute from his mouth as she smashed her lips against his, pushing with her legs as if to climb into his body. Doran had spied on his brother with a girl once, so he knew something of what to do, but Amilee took him for a ride.

He held on to her, simultaneously aroused and put off by her aggression. He'd thought her a virgin; coy as a spring flower, maybe; but still a virgin.

Amilee turned her back as she tightened the lacings to secure her bodice. A red bruise marred her shoulder where he had bitten her. She fiddled with her sleeve to cover it but the fabric slid down after each attempt and the bruise peeked over the edge of the linen, like a red fox at the entrance of its den. Her bosom trembled as she sniffled.

"What's wrong?" he said.

She turned to him and her eyes filled with tears. One spilled over her lashes and streaked down her plump cheek. Never had she looked so beautiful and vulnerable, no longer the teasing flirt perpetually out of reach. He wanted to feel her again. He sat up and reached for her shoulder. Amilee slapped his hand away, striking his wrist so hard that he yelped. She jumped to her feet, pulled up her skirt, and dashed through the birch trees toward the road.

Doran rubbed the red mark on his wrist, wondering what he had done wrong. When he saw the bag of onions, he cursed himself and the girl. How long? The sun had passed noontime. His mother would be furious if she wanted those onions for supper, and she would tell his father to use a switch on him.

He took three long strides through the birches, stopped, cursed, and came rushing back to find his flute among the crushed wildflowers.

No smoke rose from the chimney as he approached the cottage. Very odd for midday. A sick sense of dread ushered away his fears of punishment when he stopped before the partially open door, hanging idly from its hinges. No talking, no clatter, no noise at all spilled from the house.

He pushed the door and it creaked. He had never heard it creak before, had never opened the door to silence. He stepped inside and let loose the bag of onions, which thudded on the floor. One rolled out and stopped against his brother's arm. His family lay across the floor boards, their faces swollen and purple, their eyes bulging. An acrid smell fouled the room and wisps of yellow smoke wavered in the sunlight streaming through the windows. His eyes burned and he doubled over coughing.

He backed out the door and tripped, falling over and tumbling away from the cottage. As he lay on his stomach retching, he felt the flute against his breastbone...the flute that he'd found beside the woodpile, beside the hemlock wood.

Sutter's Well

"You go on in and tell him what you told us." Tom and his father stood on the weathered boardwalk outside the Sheriff's office. Tom's father wore a helmet with a lamp affixed to the front and carried a shiny lunch bucket.

"What if he don't believe me," said Tom.

The man pressed his lips together with grim determination. His clean-shaven face was pale and washed, not like it would be when he came home, smudged and black. "Ain't nothing wrong with telling the truth. It's up to others to believe. Tell him what you saw and did." The man slapped Tom on the back as he turned away and strode toward the mine.

Tom watched his father until he rounded a bend and disappeared behind the mining company store. The door handle beckoned like a hand offered. He couldn't run home. His mother would bring him right back and his father would give him a switching. The Sheriff had already talked to the doctor. Jumping into the water after Hank, into the creek with that *thing*, he was beginning to think, was easier.

"Is that you out there, Tom?"

The Sheriff's voice struck him like cold spring water to his face. "Yes, sir." He tugged the handle of the screen door, which always swelled and stuck in the spring.

TOM AND HANK TOPPED Dead Mule Ridge with the morning sun warming their backs. Each boy carried a metal bucket—paint-chipped and rusted—and over their shoulders bamboo fishing poles bounced with their steps. A cord of rope cinched their patched and mended trousers whose hems stopped well above the boys' ankles. They would outgrow the pants long before their mothers would allow them to fall apart. They wore no shoes and black dirt outlined the edges of their toenails.

For the last thirty yards the trail to the crest rose sharply and to conserve their breath for the climb, the boys had stopped talking about their brothers and sisters and the endless chores their mothers devised to keep their idle hands out of the devil's influence. They shivered as they plunged into the shade of the ridge's shadow among the pines whose needles still dripped with the morning dew. Like their grandfathers and fathers, they were destined for the coal shafts and their subconscious shuddered at any sudden withdrawal from the sun.

In the narrow valley below, little more than a crevice between the ancient mounds of rock, Whipahonic Creek splashed over stones in a slashing white fury stoked with spring rains and snowmelt. Only Tom's grandmother remembered a winter so furious with snow, but all the men had found extra work digging out trains caught in snow drifts, a rare chance to ply their shovels under the bright sky instead of the dark mountains.

"The water's high alright," said Tom.

"John Roy said last week that you couldn't see the stones."

"Sutter's Well's gonna be chock brimming with fish," said Tom.

The boys raced down the trail to the base of the ridge, flying over the ground falling beneath them. Pebbles tumbled in their wake. At the creek's edge, they picked their way among flat stones as the water rushed past in foamy white stripes and stretched over smooth rocks poking just above the surface. Twigs and branches packed together in lines along the banks marked the high water of the floods. The boys stepped around a dead trout swarming with flies, its desiccated eye caved in. The water gave and the water took, without thought or conscience.

A low rumble thrummed through the mountain rock and vibrated through their feet. Tom looked askance at Hank.

"My Pa said they're blastin' a new shaft."

Tom nodded. He imagined the mountains as hollow as honeycombs and wondered if someday the mining shafts would all cave in and the mountains would collapse into the earth in heaps of black dust and rock. Tom had told Hank his fears one day, about the tunnels falling in. Hank got older that day or maybe Tom grew younger. A man didn't say he feared such things. Every morning when his mother told him to look for chicken eggs under the porch, Tom steeled his nerves and wriggled through the dirt in the tight places beneath the porch. His mother needed the extra eggs and someone had to find them.

The water slowed and spread out as the boys descended the valley toward Sutter's Well, a deep hollow before a mile of cataracts. The bole of a long-dead tree—its bark stripped and the wood blanched and cracked—had lodged across the creek in rocks above the water line, a testament to the flood's power. The boys tottered across the natural bridge, their arms outstretched for balance, with the cold mountain water whirling beneath them.

Another rumble troubled the earth.

"What's that?" Hank pointed at the creek bed. "I never seen nothin' like that before."

Tom laid his bucket and pole amidst the rocks and joined Hank craning over the edge of the creek.

A rose-colored slab of granite flecked with black lay embedded in the slaty creek bed. Gravel and river rocks obscured the slab's rounded edges, which suggested a disk. Carved stick figures—part human and part animal: birdmen with hooked beaks, fishmen with spikes along their backs, wolfmen with fangs—spiraled over the granite surface. Other marks, possibly letters, bearing no anthropomorphic reference that the boys knew, marched with the bestiary.

"Must've been the Indians," said Tom.

"Ain't no Indians around here made things like that." Hank stepped into the water, which soaked his pant legs to above his knees. He thrust his arm into the current until his fingers touched the granite. "It's polished. Smooth as glass."

"My sister says they make some strange sculptures at that artist's colony," Tom said.

"You think they'd dump this in the creek? That place is way down the valley and this thing's bigger than a wagon wheel." Hank rocked forward and back, following the symbol's circular progression with his gaze.

Ten yards downstream, the surface of Sutter's Well rippled. Tom jerked his head toward the movement. The creek bed widened around the Well and sloped gently from the bank before plunging into a dark blue pit. No one knew its depth. No one had a rope long enough. The water's surface rolled as thick and smooth as molasses toward the first cataract. Eddies spun beside rocks. Sunlight that filtered through the trees dappled the Well's surface.

Fish after a bug, Tom decided. *And a big one.* He turned back to Hank who rocked in a circle, rotating at his hips. His gaze followed the swirling march of the half-beast half-men. His lips moved, mumbling a silent chant.

"Hey, Hank. You okay?"

Nothing. Hank raised his hands like the faithful at chapel.

Tom stepped back, an instinctual fear boiling up as the familiar metamorphosed into the weird. "Hank? This ain't funny, Hank."

Still nothing.

Tom's breath trembled. The shadows of the forest deepened and grew together, squeezing the dappled sunlight to slivers of gray on the dark water. The black clouds of a squall spread over the valley, curling around the mountain tops, gripping the peaks. The clouds rolled above like a black ceiling, like coal seams under the mountains weighing on him, shutting out the sun. He wanted to run. His body told him to flee. Nothing would have been easier than racing into the trees, but his conscience, or whatever bound him to his friend, wouldn't move.

Another fish, or something, broke the surface in the shallows on the opposite bank and then sank to the slaty rocks.

Tom gasped. He held his breath without thinking. The thing in the water looked to be the length of a man but like a crayfish with a back and tail of mottled gray fading to white. A row of black, almond shapes spread across its back in a half circle and from a bulbous ganglia at the tip of its tapered head protruded three pairs of feelers that twitched beneath the water. Two rows of white, spongy appendages held it to the river stones against the current.

Hank rocked to a rhythm inside his head. Tom sensed the rhythm too, but only faintly, like it came from another valley. He didn't hear it so much as felt it, recalling its memory from beyond his consciousness. The beast, the giant crayfish without pincers, scuttled across the creek and stopped before the disk. The shorter feelers caressed the granite while the longest ones wrapped around Hank's ankles.

"Hank!" Tom screamed. He grabbed his metal bucket by the rim and launched it at Hank, overhead, like the big-league pitchers on the radio. The bucket's lower rim thumped the back of Hank's head.

"What the hell was that for?" Hank stood tall as he turned, the spell broken. The bucket landed with a splash in the shallows.

"Look." Tom pointed at the creature at Hank's feet.

The beast flicked its tail and Hank went down before he could cry out. His back hit the surface in a spray of white water that reached up the bank to Tom's feet. Hank's head went under then bobbed on the surface, above and below. He sucked in water and air, sputtering and hacking as the beast dragged him. He grasped at stones, but the rounded rocks, slick with moss, eluded his grip. Others tumbled with him, rolled with the current toward the pit with no bottom.

Tom didn't think. One acts or stares or runs when confronted with terror, and whatever held him steady before now propelled him into the purling water. He leaped from the sloping bank to the granite disk, felt the gouges in the carved stone under his toes, and flew over the creek like an angel with outstretched arms. He touched Hank's elbow as he hit the water. Hank slipped away but not before Tom cinched his fingers around Hank's wrist.

The beast jerked them downstream. Water piled around Tom's mouth and nose as his body plowed through the creek, his deadweight adding no hindrance to the beast. Hank thrashed his free arm and bucked to raise his head and gasp some air. Tom pressed his knees into the stony creek bed, searching for leverage, all the while keeping his tenuous grip on Hank's wrist, but the beast pulled him off balance with each flick of its tail, plunging Tom's face into the chilly water. The knees of his trousers ripped and his skin tore as it scraped along the stones. A red slick of blood ebbing from Hank's ankles drifted in the current. As he struggled to gauge the distance to the Well, Tom saw the feelers for what they were, tentacles armed with bony, serrated edges.

Hank's fingers wrapped Tom's wrist, compressing flesh against bone, as a blue shadow beneath the water yawned ahead of them. They would die or live together and the thought threw Tom into a panicked frenzy of kicking and swinging as the beast jerked him beneath the water again and again.

His flailing hand caught the sharp edge of a rock. Nothing more than luck. He braced his forearm against the flat surface and when the beast pulled, Tom kept his face above the surface. He sucked in a breath and dug his knees between stones.

The beast pulled in short jerks. Tom's arms ached. He gritted his teeth and closed his eyes against the pain that shot through his shoulders as the bones strained in their sockets.

Some screams originate only in terror, others only in pain. Hank's bore the marks of both and his cry echoed through the valley, ricocheting off the ridges. Hank's arm went slack as the body lurched into Tom. Blood trailed from Hank's feet and then sank into Sutter's Well. Whatever had held Hank was gone. Tom scrambled up the bank, dragging Hank behind him. Hank coughed and spit up water that dripped off his chin.

Tom called his friend's name. Hank's eyes fluttered open and then snapped shut as another round of coughs racked his chest and water gushed from his mouth and nose. Tom turned Hank on his side. He pried Hank's cold fingers loose from around his wrist and found a blue and purple bruise in the shape of four fingers and a thumb. His hand tingled as numbness gave way to pain.

"We got away, Hank. We got away." Hank groaned and coughed, weakly at first, but then stronger as the coughs came from a deeper recess. Tom glanced at Hank's feet and turned away at once. The boy who had seen hogs butchered and deer gutted wretched his grits into a clump of knee-high grass. Strips of flesh clung to the white bones of Hank's feet and ankles.

A few drops of rain spotted the back of Tom's neck. He coughed and spat the bile from his mouth. He had to hurry before the trail over the ridge disintegrated to slick mud.

"WAS RIGHT THERE," SAID Tom. He stood at the water's edge, pointing at the gray stones in the creek bed. He resisted the urge to wade into the water and move the loose stones covering what he knew lay beneath. Fear anchored him to the land.

The Sheriff rubbed his chin and fanned his face with his hat. Sweat beaded on his forehead and gathered above his eyebrows. His paunch hung over his belt.

"People been fishin' here for years, boy, and ain't no one seen any rocks with writing."

"That *thing* must have covered it over." He shuddered, imagining those feelers shifting the rocks to cover its trap.

The Sheriff frowned, replaced his hat, straightened it. "I don't know what you saw, but it ain't here now. I think Hank got his feet wedged under some sharp rocks and you pulled him out. That was a good thing you did carrying him over the mountain."

"And why won't he talk no more?"

The Sheriff squeezed Tom's shoulder. "Let it go, boy." The Sheriff sauntered upstream, making for the trailhead.

Tom walked downstream, training a wary eye on the purling water. The blue pit yawned below him or was it an eye that watched him. The edges were shadowed, indistinct, black bleeding into gray but definitely circular, like the granite disk. A dead leaf—brown and stiff—borne atop the current, passed over the dark circle, spun around an eddy and then disappeared over a ledge of falling water.

Jump. Tom turned back to the pit. Something called, insinuating the idea of jumping into his conscious thoughts. In his mind's eye, he saw himself leaping up and over and into the Well. *Jump.* He felt the voice, like the rumble of blasting in the mountain, shaking through his legs and rattling up his spine. He felt its weight, like the joists in the porch scratching his shoulder blades, like the heat in August oppressing him, pinning him down. His feet shuffled toward the edge. Something watched him from the Well. Something held his gaze that he couldn't see through the shadowed water. *Jump.*

"Tom!" A muffled voice from far away called his name. "Boy!" The Sheriff grabbed Tom's shoulder. Tom shivered to his core. "You get any closer and you're gonna fall in. Come on."

Tom fell in behind the Sheriff. He watched the Well over his shoulder, expecting a ripple on the surface from the beast's mottled back. He watched until the trees closed in and hid the creek from view. *Never again,* he told himself. *I'm not going there ever again.* Something old lived down Sutter's Well. Something ancient.

Morphine and Chocolate

"I'm going to look for Pearl," he said.

"At this hour?" his wife asked.

"I heard about a guy who might know something. A Mr. Dire. The guy who runs the diner knows him."

She stared at her husband, shaking her head. "That's a fool's errand, Abram. And you know it."

Abram let the screen door slam, not resigned to the worst, not until he saw it. He walked downtown in the summer's dusk, trampling weeds in the cracks of the broken sidewalk. Trees thick with decades arched over his path. He remembered when Pearl rode in her red wagon beneath those trees to the ice cream shop. She wanted bubblegum ice cream, always, all pink and sugary. One day she said she could walk there like a big girl and then one day he could not recall their last trip. He remembered the day she learned to ride a bicycle, when he let go of the seat and she rode away from him on her own, screaming with excitement but too inexperienced to use her brakes. She turned into a yard and crashed in a patch of pachysandra. He remembered taking her to school, watching her crowd through the double doors with the others, all suited with brightly colored backpacks. Memories of leave taking, those alone remained crisp, crowding out all others. "I've lost my Pearl," he mumbled.

He stopped beneath a neon sign jutting out over the sidewalk from a two storey brick facade. The white letters spelled The Big Feast Diner, but the letter "e" in the third word flickered on and off so the sign sometimes read The Big Fast Diner. Light spilled from the floor to ceiling windows, casting shadows of parking meters on the vacant street.

The bell over the door chirped. A wave of cool air refreshed him as he made for the counter, striding across the black and white tile floor, past an old man drinking black coffee as he scanned a newspaper, past a young couple—all smiles and giggles—crowded together over an enormous chocolate fudge sundae.

A chubby, balding man in a white shirt and apron smiled at him from behind the counter. "Lookin' for Mr. Dire?"

Abram nodded as he raised himself onto a seat. To his right three identical girls perched on stools. Their platinum blond hair shook in unison when they glanced at him.

He stretched his arms and back, pausing a moment to peek at the girls who wore identical clothes, long-sleeved pink dresses that clung without being obscene. Their pleated skirts reminded him of cheerleader outfits. Darker pink tights covered their legs which ended in pink, high-top tennis shoes. Their hair stopped abruptly at their shoulders and their bangs brushed their eyebrows. They shared a banana split drenched with chocolate sauce.

"The Triplets," said the Proprietor. "The same but different. Don't think I've ever heard them disagree. That's gotta make you wonder."

"Yup." Abram stuck his elbows on the polished black counter top and massaged his forehead.

"Can I get you something?"

"Maybe a coffee. With some cream."

"You should try the ice cream," chorused the Triplets. "The chocolate sauce is divine." They smiled.

"The ladies don't lie," said the Proprietor.

Their unitary behavior unnerved him, as did the Proprietor's nonchalance. Pink and ice cream triggered the memories, sparking a short circuit in his head, a wall of fuzzy images like so many televisions going bad, their pictures losing sharpness as Pearl faded into the depths of half-remembered dreams.

Don't dwell on it. Don't snivel and sob.

He was losing her, a bit more everyday, and nothing filled the void. He carried a school picture in his wallet from years ago, its white edges worn. She was all smiles and hope against some blue, grainy background like granite, like the polished stone of a grave marker.

Abram steadied his voice, which still squeaked. "Just the coffee, please."

The Proprietor nodded, fixing his lips in a firm line. The Triplets rolled their eyes then huddled together in a cloud of whispers. Abram stirred the cream into his coffee, watching the black fade to muddy amber.

"Here he comes," announced the Proprietor.

Something banged against the door and screeched, metal against metal. The bell chirped. A rolling squeak built to a crescendo then faded and rolled out again.

Everyone swiveled to the door.

Crouched in a narrow wooden box mounted on a hospital gurney, a man pushed his way into the diner, using a crutch as one paddles a canoe. Black sunglasses hid his eyes. Black, curly locks flared out beneath a red baseball cap worn backwards, and in his mouth he clenched the end of the longest, thickest joint that Abram had ever seen.

Mr. Dire stopped halfway between the door and the counter. He sucked air through his cannabis cigar, which crackled and flared red. Thick white smoke seeped from his lips and nose, like an incense burner, shrouding his face.

"Anyone got an ash tray?" said Mr. Dire.

The Proprietor reminded Mr. Dire of the city ordinance that prohibited smoking in restaurants.

"Oh." Mr. Dire chuckled. "Forgot." He tapped his cigar on the edge of the pine box. A clump of ash splattered on a white tile. Other bits floated to the floor like tiny gray snow flakes.

The Triplets wrinkled their noses. The old man returned to his paper and coffee. The young man held his girl's hand, kissing a green, plastic ring on her finger, something from a cereal box. The young woman giggled. Abram waited for the Proprietor to make an introduction but none came.

Mr. Dire took another drag on his cannabis. "I hear somebody lost something." Puffs of smoke accented each word, hanging between Mr. Dire and Abram.

"I did. I've lost my Pearl."

"Well, I'm good—" Mr. Dire's voice cracked. He cleared his throat. "Good at finding lost things." His voice trailed to a raspy gurgle. He coughed, deep and wet, then spat black phlegm on the floor.

The Triplets turned away. Abram felt his stomach lurch.

"Now I've got to clean that up," said the Proprietor. He wheeled a mop and bucket from behind the counter.

Mr. Dire inhaled a long hit. "Come with me and we'll find your Pearl."

Abram slid off the stool and took a step toward Mr. Dire and his gurney boat. The nearest Triplet gripped his arm.

"Don't go," she said.

"Finding Pearl is all that matters. If I have to go with him to do it, I will."

"You won't find what you're looking for. There's another path."

"I've tried everything imaginable. Everyone's given up except me. If she's out there, God help me, I'll find her."

He wrenched his arm from the Triplet. She let him go.

"Climb in," said Mr. Dire.

Abram stepped on a chair and clambered behind Mr. Dire into the box, a long box that narrowed toward its head and foot, an antique casket.

"You can help push," said Mr. Dire, handing him a crutch. "But first I gotta get you hooked up." He reached behind Abram for some plastic tubing attached to an IV bag hanging from a pole mounted on the gurney. Holding his cigar in his mouth, Mr. Dire pushed up Abram's sleeve and twisted his arm, exposing the green veins on its underside. He tightened his cold grip, steadying the patient.

"What are you doing?" Abram jerked to wrest back his arm, but Mr. Dire's fingers coiled tighter.

Mr. Dire mumbled behind his cigar. "You're gonna need this where we're going. This is gonna hurt but not for long." He plunged a needle into a vein.

Abram cried out at the sharp jab, then a swell rolled over him, dampening all his pain, washing it away like a sandcastle on a beach under successive waves. He felt Mr. Dire apply tape to his IV, an abstract procedure connected to his consciousness by only the thinnest of threads.

His thoughts snapped back into clarity.

They rolled along an asphalt road cutting straight across a vast scrub plain. Clumps of yellowed grass, gnarled trees, and tumble weeds dotted the land of dry, reddish dirt that faded to black at the horizons. Yellow clouds tinged with amber covered the sky, exploding downward in great billowy spikes, sucking material from yawning clefts, before recoiling as the jutting cloud collapsed. Sepia washed the air like some sulfurous smog. No sound disturbed the land except the squeaking gurney wheel and the crutch paddle tapping the pavement.

"Where are we?" he said.

He startled when Mr. Dire jerked around to face him. A breathing mask covered his nose and mouth with the ever present cannabis cigar stuck in the hole reserved for an oxygen tube. Wispy tentacles of smoke crept from the mask's edges and slithered across his face and neck.

Mr. Dire put down his crutch, pulled down his mask, and spread his arms, signifying the vast expanse of waste. "The place of lost things."

"We'll find Pearl here?"

"She's just up the road."

Mr. Dire resumed paddling. Abram joined in with vigor. Each jab and push brought him closer to his little girl. He was going to find Pearl, prove them all wrong. Liquid dripped from the IV bag through the tube to the needle embedded in his arm.

They stopped when the road dead-ended at the edge of a field colored with red poppies.

"There she is," said Mr. Dire.

Ten paces in front of them, nestled amid the red flowers, stood a blowup doll, naked, its legs splayed. An image of Pearl, her auburn hair cascading over her shoulders, decorated the balloon.

"What?" cried Abram.

"Are you gonna go see her?"

"It's a blowup sex toy, you jackass."

"It's what's inside." Mr. Dire fiddled with a tie on the tubing. "Now you've got some slack. Go look."

Abram climbed down to the road, crushing flowers underfoot as he approached the doll. The plastic tether to the IV bag trailed behind him, unwinding. He touched her smiling face, nothing more than cold vinyl, an obscene, lifeless duplicate.

"You'll need this," said Mr. Dire. He tossed a crutch to Abram. "Press the button by the handle."

A scythe blade snapped out the side of the crutch.

"Now they can't see me coming," shouted Mr. Dire.

Abram jabbed the blow-up doll's stomach with the scythe. Air gushed out, whining as the doll crumpled over the flowers. He looked askance at Mr. Dire.

"Look, man. Feel around in the legs."

Abram stuck his hand inside the plastic shell, down one leg and then the other. Something round and hard rolled about.

He pinched it between his fingers and brought it out, a smooth, black sphere in his cupped palm.

"See?" Mr. Dire laughed as he spoke. "You found your little pearl."

Abram hurled the pearl, grunting with the effort. It bounced off Mr. Dire's chest onto the road and then rolled back into the poppy field. Screaming expletives, he ripped the IV needle from his arm, tearing skin and pulling hair. Blood pulsed from the wound, trailing down his arm. Mr. Dire laughed on and on. Abram charged at him with the scythe and with one stroke severed the man's head. A fountain of black blood spurted from the decapitated torso. Mr. Dire's head landed on the road where it wobbled. The cigar still protruded from its mouth, clenched between its teeth.

"It's a gusher," cried the head, followed by more laughter.

Abram threw the scythe to the pavement. He cocked one leg back and then kicked the head like a soccer ball. It sailed high, arching over the poppy field.

"Score, score," shouted the head as it flew.

Abram charged into the poppy field, intending to kick and batter the head to mush. A furrow caught his foot, sending him face first into the dirt and flowers.

He thrashed in the clear light of the diner, the black and white tiles beneath him. When fingers touched his shoulder, he twisted onto his back to find one of the Triplets leaning over him, extending her hand.

"Welcome back," she said.

Abram grasped her fingers. The fight left him, pushed out as peace surged from her touch. Strength hid behind her thin appearance. She pulled him to his feet with little effort.

He mumbled thanks.

"You're bleeding," said the Triplet.

Blood oozed from the wound in his arm. The Proprietor said he would fix it and retrieved a white tackle box marked with a red cross. He dabbed the wound with peroxide and then covered it with a bandage.

"Find what you were lookin' for?" asked the Proprietor.

"No. A total waste. Did I actually go anywhere?"

"You most certainly did," said the Triplet.

"Mr. Dire claims he can find anything lost," said the Proprietor.

"I don't think Mr. Dire will be coming back."

The Proprietor chuckled. "I wouldn't bet on that."

The Triplet touched his hand. "Do you really want to know Pearl's fate?"

"What do you know about her?"

"More than you can imagine."

He looked past the Triplet to her sisters eating the banana split. "Are you some of the friends she wouldn't tell us about?"

The Triplet smiled. "I'm afraid you won't like what I have to show you."

He shrugged. "Where are we going?"

"The woods," answered the Triplet. "But first, have some chocolate."

"Comin' right up," said the Proprietor. "Premium vanilla with that special sauce."

"What's in the woods?" asked Abram. "We've already searched them with dogs."

"You'll see."

The Proprietor served him a single scoop mantled with thick chocolate sauce. "Best stuff in town."

"So I've heard." Abram turned to the Triplet. "You want me to eat this?"

She nodded.

He carved a spoonful of ice cream dripping with chocolate and let it melt in his mouth. The Proprietor and the Triplet watched him finish and scrape the chocolate sauce from the sides of the bowl.

"Okay," he said. "Now what?"

The Triplet smiled. Movement stopped. The diner stilled, captured as a painting or a photograph. The Triplet's face sank, followed by the counter, the range, the calendar on the wall. Everything lost its distinct edges, dripping and running like a watercolor left in the rain.

When his vision cleared, he stood in a forest. Sunlight filtered through the leaves and holes in the canopy. The Triplet held his hand.

"Where are we?"

"The border lands of paradise." She dropped his hand and pointed ahead of them. "What you seek is up there."

He plodded through the undergrowth, pushing saplings aside, ducking below outstretched limbs. Ferns and bushes slapped his shins. The gurgle of rushing water grew louder. The stream sang a sweet melody, a trembling alto calling to him and he hurried in its direction.

A fallen limb, or so he thought, tripped his foot. He fell on a low mound of loose dirt and withered leaves, long dead from seasons past. As he pushed himself up, his fingers contacted the unexpected, cold flesh. A gray wrist and hand, its fingers clinched, protruded from the mound's edge.

Abram recognized the interlocking chain tattoo around the wrist, a source of so much strife between father and daughter. He pawed the mound, pushing handfuls of dirt to either side, sniffling, staunching tears with the back of his wrist. Pearl's head, neck, and naked shoulders emerged from the dirt. A partially open eye, as green as the forest leaves, stared at him. The other remained shut, a slit at the center of a purple bruise streaked with black and gray. A gash marred her nose where the killer who had stolen his little girl had ripped out her nose ring. A ligature cinched her neck.

He dug his hands beneath her shoulders, buried his face in her hair, and wept.

The Triplet touched his shoulder. "I said you wouldn't like it."

"You knew. You damned bitch." He stood, ready to beat her with all his anger.

"Look." At the end of a narrow path through the woods, a stream glittered in the sun, its rippled surface catching the light at odd angles. The air above the water shimmered and beyond the stream, a young woman waited. She wore a dress of pure white. Her auburn locks cascaded down her shoulders.

"Is it?"

"Go and see, but you may not cross the river."

He sprinted down the path. With each stride the young woman's form sharpened in his bleary eyes.

Pearl lived.

He halted at the edge of the stream, its bed strewn with sapphires, rubies, and diamonds. Pearl stood on the water's edge at the end of a path paved with white pearls. A forest spread along the stream on either side of her.

"Pearl?"

"Yes, Daddy." She looked every bit a bride on her wedding day. He expected her to spin around, letting her pearl-beaded rolls of fabric billow in circles.

"Thank heavens. I thought I'd lost you. You don't know what I've been through to find you. But what—"

"Lost me?" she said, interrupting him. "Was I yours to lose?"

"You're my daughter."

She sighed. "Do you like my dress?" She raised her arms and smiled and he saw the little girl who posed as Cinderella on a Halloween many years ago.

"Yes. It's beautiful, Pearl. But what happened? Who?" He hesitated over the words, pointing toward the shallow grave. "Did that?"

Her smile faded. "It's of little consequence to me now. Why waste our short time together?"

"Short?" He stepped forward into the stream. The water crackled and smoked at his touch. He jerked back his foot which throbbed with burning.

"You can't cross. Didn't they tell you? Your time hasn't come."

"Can you cross?"

"I was told not to."

"I just want to hold you."

"But I'm not yours to hold, Daddy."

"Try, for your father's sake, just for a few moments."

Pearl stared at the water. "I'm sorry, Daddy, but I will not disobey my Father."

"Your father? I'm your father."

"We are both children, supplicants, brother and sister, just as we are both royalty."

"That's ridiculous."

"How can I disobey Him? He has made me the queen of heaven."

"You never wanted to go to church."

Pearl frowned. "You don't approve. You never did approve. He said you wouldn't understand. How did you want to find me? Injured? In desperate need of your help?"

"No, Pearl, no. You don't understand."

"This was not about finding me. I am found. It was about *you* finding me. He's calling me. I have to go now. I love you and He loves you, too. You've been given a tremendous gift, meeting me here. Please don't waste it."

"Pearl! Don't go, please."

"I'll wait for you, mother as well, but don't hurry. We know no tomorrow or yesterday here."

Abram watched her disappear amid the trees arching over the white path. He sat down on the edge of the stream. "We argued," he said aloud to himself. "What we always do."

"It's time to go back," said the Triplet.

He slapped her hand from his shoulder. His head ached. He shut his eyes and pressed his hands to his temples. He felt himself spinning, feeling sicker. When the spinning stopped, he was sitting on the sidewalk outside the diner in the gray light of early dawn. A closed sign hung in the door.

A police car pulled to a stop near the curb. "You all right, buddy?" said the officer.

"Tired. I was looking for my daughter."

"Did you find her?"

"I think so. I don't know. Maybe."

The officer frowned at him. "Get on home. There's no loitering."

The Facts in the Case of M. Hussman

October 31, 1890

To the Science and Engineering editors at *The Chicago Times Weekly* and to all interested parties, both legal and scientific,

The bizarre events respecting the untimely deaths of Professor Arnold Hussman and his wife Cordelia have prompted a firestorm of ignorant speculation equal in destructiveness to the Great Fire. As a friend and assistant to Professor Hussman, I believe a first-hand testimony is required to counterbalance the slanderous invective tossed about as objective truth and to reaffirm my mentor's scientific credentials. The experiment was conducted in good faith and with the most noble intentions. Scientific progress often wends through dark forests and over crags. It is not the pursuit of the timid, and one can hardly fault a husband for loving his wife too much.

For fifteen years Cordelia Hussman stood by her husband's side, from the early days when family questioned her choice of a man with dreams but few prospects to the wild success of his later inventions. Her family connections with bankers and investors procured the capital so essential to Professor Hussman's projects. I knew her only briefly through my association with Professor Hussman and the many suppers I shared in their dining room. She held her own in any conversation, employing her formidable wit and impeccable manners, and I daresay beneath that veneer of beauty and breeding that she could be as single-minded and "ruthless" as Hussman, himself.

As attested by the eminent Doctors Laslow and Dunbarton, Mrs. Hussman suffered the wasting disease, and with great sadness we watched as eight months ago she entered that affliction's final stages. Her lips and extremities assumed a bluish hue, her breathing slowed to intermittent gurgling gasps, and her eyes lost their moist luster, remaining open or closed for hours at a time. Her heart fluttered so faintly that only the most sensitive stethoscope could detect its pulsing. It is unbearably cruel that the world should be deprived of such a woman in the prime of her life, but Professor Hussman did not wring his hands at her bedside. The master engineer and his assistant had much to do.

Many of your readers are doubtless familiar with the celebrated case of M. Valdemar in which a man near death was mesmerized. For several months he persisted in a mesmeric sleep and the decay of his body was thwarted although Valdemar exhibited no signs of vitality save a vibrating, swollen tongue. Suspended in time, his corpus remained in a steady state until a disastrous attempt to awaken him occasioned instantaneous decomposition. Hussman and Dunbarton theorized that failure to maintain Valdemar's tissue doomed the experiment.

"If there is anything, anything at all that we can do to thwart death's greed," Hussman confided to me. "We will do it."

We labored day and night for a month. I don't know when the man took rest or sustenance. When we were not pouring over diagrams or grinding and fitting metal pieces, he sat with Cordelia, comforting her with poetry: Shelley, Byron, whatever came to hand. One of Hussman's miniature steam engines, with a dual hairspring redundancy, powered the life-giving machine: a two-piston pump to mimic the heart and a bellows to inflate and deflate the lungs. I daresay a machine of such intricacy, precision, and power has never been seen and with the passing of such genius will not likely come to light again in the near future.

As her increasingly stertorous breathing knelled death's approach, Dunbarton, Hussman, and I gathered round her bed in an upper chamber on the west wing of Hussman's mansion. The white washed walls and scrubbed floor smelt of carbolic acid and ethyl alcohol and was the polar opposite of the rich and varied wallpapers that decorated the rest of the house. A shared anxiety, like static electricity, crackled among us. Dunbarton's previous attempts at mesmerizing Cordelia had failed. This would be the last attempt.

Dunbarton fixed his gaze on her fading eyes and passed his hands above her body, first along its length from head to toe and then across her abdomen and chest, repeating the passes until her eyes glazed over and followed him. If the reader has ever witnessed a snake charmer, he will have a ready example for comparison. Dunbarton raised each of her arms without the merest physical touch as if the thinnest thread of silk connected them to his will. He closed her eyes with a mere pass of his hands above her face.

"She was very receptive today," Dunbarton said.

Hussman knelt beside the bed and clasped her hand in both of his. "A good sign, yes?"

Dunbarton frowned. "Her strength has ebbed. She may have been resisting on previous attempts. Are you asleep, Cordelia?"

We waited. Dunbarton repeated the query.

A raspy hiss emanated from her parted lips. "Yes."

Hussman kissed her hand as if his most ardent prayer had been answered.

"Cordelia, are you prepared to continue?" asked Dunbarton.

Another raspy hiss. "Die."

"No, darling," said Hussman. "We're going to cheat death with whatever is in my power. Have faith. This can be done."

Dunbarton glanced at me, his brow furrowed and his lips set in a decisive frown. He shooed the nurses out into the hall and took Hussman to the far corner of the sick room out of my earshot. An animated but hushed conversation ensued. I know from experience that Hussman can be stubborn and single minded, such is the character of inventive genius.

Hussman turned from Dunbarton and ordered me to attach and ready the machine.

"You are making a mistake," said Dunbarton. "Her will is not with us."

"That is your learned opinion and I respect it," countered Hussman. "But with respect to the feelings of my wife, I think I know them better than you."

Dunbarton shook his head. "Nothing clouds a man's judgment like the death of a loved one."

"I concede your point, but we will proceed with or without you. My friend, we have little hope without your help. Please. I implore you to stay."

I stood with the bellows in hand, awaiting instruction. Dunbarton and Hussman stared at one another. Would all our work on the machine be for nothing? Would Cordelia slip away without a fight? After an interminable period of silence, Dunbarton nodded.

Hussman inserted a copper tube attached to the bellows into his wife's trachea. I attached tubes to vessels in her arm to draw and push blood through the pump and back into her body and then readied the machine's boiler while Hussman sat with his wife, clasping her hand as her body's functions slowed to a stop. Dunbarton stood at the foot of the bed, watching us work.

Cordelia Hussman's case progressed much as Valdemar's although attempts to elicit further speech failed, perhaps a result of the tracheotomy. Hussman found that his wife could communicate by gently squeezing his hand. As with Valdemar, the mesmeric sleep slowed her decline. She responded to questions from Dunbarton and Hussman after working out a code of two squeezes for yes and one for no. She answered that her approaching death brought no discomfort. As the end neared, only a ticking clock and the sporadic hiss of steam from the boiler disturbed the pregnant silence that suffused the sickroom.

After hours of vigil, Mrs. Hussman's lower jaw slackened and her tongue pushed between her lips. Dunbarton found no pulse or heartbeat. He repeated his question three times before

Cordelia's arm trembled, apparently summoning its last bit of strength, and confirmed her death.

One of the nurses swooned. I set the engine in motion at Hussman's command. The bellows rose and fell as did Mrs. Hussman's chest. Blood flowed from her arm and back into it. Almost immediately a rosy blush drove the pallor from her cheeks as a spark of her former loveliness took hold. The effect was nothing short of miraculous. Her eyes remained closed and she responded only to the questions of Dunbarton, but warmth, reported Hussman, had spread through her hand which now gripped with living strength.

For six weeks we tended her, sleeping on cots and keeping vigil in shifts. Only a solitary, daily stroll through the back garden, Cordelia's pride and joy, relieved our strain. If only we could have taken Cordelia to the garden, but such a move was impossible. I monitored the machine and stoked the boiler. Dunbarton inserted a tube down her throat at intervals to provide broth. How long she might have persisted in this state of conscious, post-death vitality seemed unbounded. At Hussman's direction, Dunbarton relayed news of family and friends. I admit excitement inhibited my judgment and that of Hussman. We should have given more attention to the clear discharge draining from the corners of her eyes, which Dunbarton likened to tears.

On the forty-third day following her death, her mouth closed so tightly that Dunbarton could not feed her. The three of us gathered, fearing that some contagion had stiffened her facial muscles. To all queries she answered no, gripping with enough strength to crack Hussman's knuckles.

"Tell her I love her with all my heart and mind," implored Hussman.

Dunbarton relayed the message. Cordelia squeezed once.

"My love," said Hussman.

"You are not content," said Dunbarton.

No.

Still gripping his wife's hand, Hussman doubled over and pressed his eyes to his forearm, ineffectually hiding his sobs.

"Do you wish to die?" asked Dunbarton.

Yes.

"No," shouted Hussman. Everyone in the room, so focused on the patient, startled at his outburst. "No, darling. No. Not yet." His eyes flashed with the wild intensity of a rabid beast. I thought for a moment that I didn't know him, that he had succumbed to the strain of his despair. He fell on her breast to smother her face in kisses.

Where she found the strength, we know not, but her arm snapped over her husband's shoulders, pressing his neck to her face. Her movement disconnected a tube. I slipped on the floorboards slick with blood pulsing from the pump. Hussman cried out in a scream that terminated in a hideous gurgle. With the help of two nurses, Dunbarton freed Hussman from his wife's preternatural grip. Blood, Professor Hussman's blood, streamed from Cordelia's mouth down her cheeks. Her eyes, closed for so many weeks, were now open, staring at the unornamented, white ceiling. The nurses ran shrieking from the room. I stopped my efforts with the machine. Blood splashed on the floor behind me, draining from Cordelia. In his arms, Dunbarton held the limp remains of Professor

Hussman, whose dead wife had ripped his throat with her teeth.

Respectfully, etc.
Cornelius Direbrand

Shafts to Hell

"Now you listen carefully." He poked a stubby, calloused finger at his audience sitting on the bunk across the cell. "It didn't happen the way they've been tellin' it. Can't say who could put up with all Elmore's preachin'. All shut up in the bowels of that gold mine. Those tunnels were tighter than a snake skin, and the deeper we dug and blasted, the tighter they got."

He shivered. "Gives me the willies just to tell of it. Like coffins they were, all dark and dusty and narrow, my neck scratching the rock above and my chin the rock below, and Elmore behind me jawin' on and on about sin and kingdom come. All the while we were diggin' our way to Hell."

He laughed. "Elmore wasn't always so high and mighty. I wouldn't have made him my partner if I'd known how marryin' that Bible-thumpin' teetotaler would tarnish him. The whores weren't good enough for Elmore. No, he had to have himself some kind of lady, somethin' pretty and shiny. I'll admit she was a fine woman to look at. Don't know what she wanted with Elmore. Maybe she saw something malleable, like gold.

"If only we'd struck a big vein before, well, before he took to preachin'. I know it's there. We'd see glimmers of it, streaks of yellow like Elsie's hair and that yellow dress she wore on

Sundays." He shook his head. "Sundays. Elmore quit workin' on Sundays after gettin' hitched to Elsie. Left me to do all the diggin' myself. But it wasn't all bad, alone every seventh day. Some folks go to hear preachin' on Sundays. That's the only day I *didn't* hear preachin'. And I'm thankful.

"Was on a Sunday that I got stuck. Got my gut wedged in tight and Elmore wasn't there to pull me out. My candle burnt itself out and I was trapped in the darkest of mines. Any direction I moved my hands or arms, I hit rock. I shivered and screamed but that mountain had a grip on me. That mine wailed when the wind blew, and all night I lay in the black guts of the earth, listenin' to the mine wail. I've heard people say that moanin' is from the souls stuck in Hell, cryin' for mercy. Well, if that be true, they begged all night and didn't get none.

"Guess I'll find out for myself soon enough. As Elmore was so fond of sayin', I got more sin weighin' on my head than the mountain above the mine. Ain't no way I'm gettin' into heaven. No, siree. I done cooked my goose. But I shivered all night, surrounded by all that cold rock, fearin' a scorpion might crawl up my pants. Elmore pulled me out in the mornin', tied a rope round my ankles."

He leaned against the wall, stroking the ragged beard covering his chin, grinning at the opposite bunk. "I bet you're wantin' to know why I did it, where I got the idea. Well one day we got to talkin' about sin and flesh and those folks that got snowed in, the Donner people, and had to eat their dead to make it through the winter. Elmore mounted his high horse and said he would starve to death before he'd.... Now what did he say? 'Violate the sanctity of a fella's remains.' That got me to thinkin', in that twisted way you think when you been crawlin' around beneath the mountains.

"Wasn't too hard really. You could say lady luck paid me a visit. Elsie was takin' the stage to San Francisco, to visit her sister. I asked her to come by my shack and take some letters to mail. Elmore went on up to the mine. She was gussied up real pretty. Her being a trusting, Christian woman, never crossed her mind why I'd have letters since my ma and pa are long dead and I've got no notion of where my brothers are. I didn't go up to the mine that day. I was busy.

"When Elmore came down the mountain, I told him we had a feast. He thought I'd butchered a hog, but no siree, there ain't nothing that'd make me kill one of my fatted barrows to feed Elmore, even to celebrate the mother vein. So we sat down and ate our fill of meat and Elmore smiled his stupid grin and patted his swollen belly. The only thing worse than his preachin' was his damned optimism. He always thought we were just one pickax swing from the mother vein. That's why he pushed me to work so long and to squeeze into places where a man ain't fit to squeeze. It was greed, cold as the snow on top of the mountain.

"'Well,' I asked him after he'd stuffed his fat belly, 'what'd you think of the meat?' He said it was the sweetest pork he'd ever tasted. Now it was my turn to grin. I went over to the stove and took the lid off of one of the pots. I was pickling Elsie's head in some moonshine. Served that teetotaler right to soak up some real lightnin' and fire. I grabbed Elsie's head by the hair and held it up for Elmore to see. 'Say hello to your dinner,' I said.

"Things got a bit confused after that. Somehow Elmore got a knife stuck in his chest. He loved that little woman so much that he tried to cut open his stomach to let her out, but he wasn't letting her out of me. Some people been sayin' that I'm a savage, but I ain't no injun. I didn't lift a scalp off Elsie and hang her locks outside my door. No, I left her pretty hair attached to her head. Folks like Elmore would starve in the mountains, but not me. I know how to—" He stopped at the sound of voices belonging to the Sheriff and a stranger.

"If not for the, well, the savagery," said the Sheriff, "it'd be your typical case of murder. One partner killing the other when they get up to a big strike. The bank manager said Elmore thought they were close, and Elmore wasn't one for counting his chickens."

"This is common?" asked the strange voice.

"The murder, not the other. These miners get greed boiling over, looking for gold one day after another."

"Greed and jealousy are the poisons of the soul."

"Shame about Elsie. Not right for an honest, respectable woman to suffer like that."

"Will I be able to spend some time alone with him?"

"That won't be a problem, Padre. No one will bunk with him. And I'm obliged to you for riding all the way over here. I'm not a cruel man so I like to honor their last request if I can."

"A lost soul was calling. The, uh, the...."

"He's gonna swing in the morning if that's what you're asking. Expect a big crowd. Elsie was much liked. The Sheriff unlocked the door to the cells. "Melvin, here's that priest you asked for."

Melvin gawked. The Priest stepped forward then stopped and stared at the bunk opposite, where a pillow sat propped against the wall with a happy face scrawled on it in black bean juice.

"Made his own bunk mate," said the Sheriff. "Talks to it all day and night long."

"I see," said the Priest, fingering the crucifix hanging over his heart.

Melvin lunged to the bars, dropping to his knees. He thrust out his arm and grabbed a handful of the Priest's black robes. The Priest flinched and tried to back away, but Melvin held fast to the cassock.

"I've sinned horribly, Father, so much that the Almighty, Jesus, and the Holy Ghost all together can't forgive me. But I need to know somethin' before I hang. Tell me, Father. Is Hell a cramped place, long and narrow, like a gold mine?"

Good King David

U zzah strode across the courtyard, angling for the double gate, the only break in the palisade. A predawn mist swirled at his ankles and a damp chill seeped through the woolen tunic beneath his leather brigandine. Two small fires crackled on either side of the path. Ash glowing red spiraled upward in the heat and smoke before burning out to black and disappearing in the night sky. Something wasn't right. He sniffed. A stench came forth from hell or the gates, metallic and musky like battle and blood but faint like a memory.

A shadow passed the gate. "Halt," shouted Uzzah. He gripped the hilt of his sword. "Who walks the King's ground without leave?"

"And who challenges the King's watchman?" the shadow answered.

"Ahio," said Uzzah. The brothers clapped each other on the shoulders and then stepped closer to one of the fires to warm their hands. "I expected to find you on the wall."

"I would be, but...."

Uzzah followed Ahio's gaze to a dark corner of the palisade blackened with shadows from the walkway overhead.

"There's something foul in the air tonight."

"Aye," said Ahio. "I came down to have a look."

They nodded to one another, drew their swords, and advanced toward the wall, following the sick scent.

"Who's there?" Ahio shouted in a tone backed with steel, a command rather than a question.

A groan answered them, a mournful, wavering note, reeking of festering wounds but very far away like the splash at the bottom of a well reverberating to the surface. The watchmen stopped their advance. That groan belonged to no mortal man or any animal they had ever slain. They held their position, fighting their instincts, forsaking a bolt for the safety of the fire because no soldier wants to be the first to flee. They waited, but whatever groaned spoke nothing more.

"Unfold yourself," said Ahio.

The mist at the base of the wall glowed yellow and swirled with streaks of red, growing taller until it reached the height of a man. The watchmen stepped backward, gaping at the spectre coalescing before them.

The translucent form—a tall man with a stout body and arms like a bear—hovered in the shadow of the wall. Clotted blood matted a yellow beard that trailed down his chest. His gray mail was torn across his shoulder. Another gash sagged above the opposite hip. Splotches of dried blood, the color of ochre, stained the tunic as if he had splashed through a river of it. No helm protected his head.

"It's Uriah," said Ahio.

"Uriah the Geat," said Uzzah.

Uriah the ghost turned his eyes to them. Once the deep blue of a glacier lake beneath a summer sun, his eyes weighed with the leaden gray of a rolling sea on the verge of a storm. With a tired, hollow voice, it spoke. "Send for Absalom."

Uzzah and Ahio exchanged nervous glances. "We should rouse Nathanael the Wise," whispered Uzzah. "He'll know the witchery at work here."

"I'll fetch him at once," said Ahio but the hollow voice stopped him.

"You believe the dead deaf? That I am a conjurer's trick? Do you not see the blood of my wounds? Shall I turn my head and show you my cleaved skull? How many curses have I lain on the hand wielding the ax that parted me from Bathsheba. A hand I would have died for without a second thought."

"'Tis not right to speak with the dead," said Ahio.

"Nor is treachery and murder," said Uriah. "You honored me once. Will you not honor me after death? Fetch Absalom."

The watchmen backed away. "If Absalom will come," said Ahio. "We will bring him."

"I shall wait," said the ghost, whose shape faded and folded in on itself, leaving a pillar of white mist.

The watchmen abandoned their post, a terrible breach for which a rope and tree awaited, but the ghost had addled their thoughts, bending them.

They found Absalom in the great hall, wrapped in elk hide blankets, sprawled on a dais before the king's table. A wolfhound with shaggy white fur lay beside him, resting its head on its paws. The sweet scent of mead punctuated here and there with the stench of vomit wafted from the stone floor. Orange embers dying in the fire pit reflected in the black pools of the hound's eyes. Its nostrils quivered, ever vigilant. It followed the movements of the watchmen as they stepped over and around snoring bodies. It growled as they approached. They gave a wide berth to the beast. According to rumor, the hound was the maker of eunuchs. Few believed the rumors, but none tested them. Uzzah knelt beside Absalom and nudged his shoulder until he stirred.

The prince squinted at them. "What? It's still night."

"We beg your forgiveness. But Uriah the Geat has come back. He demands to speak with you."

"Uriah? He's dead, you fools."

"He's come in spirit," whispered Uzzah. "He waits for you by the gate."

"In spirit?" Absalom raised his head and shoulders, leaning on his elbow, his linen shirt trimmed with silver threads at the collar and wrists. "What does Nathanael say of this?"

"We came directly to you," said Ahio as he knelt beside Uzzah. "It's Uriah. We saw the wounds."

Absalom threw off the blankets. He wrapped a bear skin cloak around his shoulders. Jabbing a finger at the hound, he commanded it to stay. The hound watched Absalom follow Uzzah and Ahio the length of the hall and into the night. It turned its nose to the thigh bone just beyond its front paws.

THE WATCHMEN STOPPED at the fires beside the path and pointed to the swirling pillar of mist that glimmered white against the shadowed wall as if a dagger of moonlight had stabbed the fog.

Absalom combed his fingers through twisted curls of his raven locks. He looked at the full moon chasing the western horizon, a single white eye behind scudding, wispy clouds.

"A trick of the moon."

"Do the moon and the fog speak?" said Uzzah.

Absalom glared at Uzzah and for a moment the two watchmen believed he growled deep and low at the back of his throat, but the night had already played tricks with their senses and they no longer trusted them.

Uzzah bowed his head. "Forgive me, sire. I swear it spoke to us."

"With enough mead and wine the moon might do anything."

"It took shape when we approached," said Ahio.

"You deserted your posts. Joab would do much worse than hang you." Absalom laughed at their ashen faces. "You still possess enough wits to fear Joab so you can't be too witless. Give me some water. If I'm to speak to a ghost I can't go with a parched throat."

Absalom drank from a gourd that Uzzah proffered, held it above his mouth with his head flung back to catch the last drops.

"Did it say it was Uriah?"

"There was no need," said Ahio.

"Uriah," shouted Absalom. "I've come."

When the pillar said nothing, Absalom leaped across the fire pit and strode toward the swirling mist.

The same groan accompanied the transformation, the cry of an agonized prisoner chained to the floor of a dry well. A snap and a spark and the pillar churned like a cyclone, spawning from the ground a man of light and shadow. The groan brought Absalom to a sudden halt. The young prince nearly fell into the translucent man.

"Uriah," said Absalom.

"What is left," said Uriah, "when all a man holds dear is slashed from him."

Absalom took a deep breath, swallowed hard, and reached for his absent hound. "To what.... I was...." He held the ghost's gaze as he fumbled for words. "You summoned me? Surely you want my father."

"Do you ask the Frisians for aid to fight the Frisians?"

"You were loyal," said Absalom. "My father did you no wrong. You were entombed with more honor than a king."

"Guilt. My honor was a salve for his guilt. How quickly he found a husband for my widow. There is a festering sore at the heart of your house; it spreads its poison through the branches, sickening the flesh with greed and lust."

"Lies and slander, you fiend. Who sent you?"

"There are some agonies that even the grave cannot contain. Idiot. Your father, our king and master, coveted my joy, seduced her into adultery, and sent me to my death."

"You're one of Baal's demons, an agent from a Jutish sorcerer sent to sow discord."

"There is no need to sow when corruption grows abundant."

"Am I to believe hearsay about your widow? Prove your charges. Show me the corruption, this pestilence spreading through my father's house."

"You have a sister, a much beloved sister."

"Tamar. Yes?"

"You shall see."

The light faded to gray shadow and the shadow to night and the ghost was no more. Absalom stared at the darkness below the wall. He heard the footfalls of the watchmen approaching from behind. He ignored them. Something prophetic had been announced, witchery against Tamar.

"Prince Absalom," said Ahio. "Was it Uriah?"

"I don't know," said Absalom. "Something malevolent. When day breaks, send Nathanael to me."

KING DAVID SAT IN A throne carved from the bole of a massive oak. Reliefs of bears and wolves spiraled around the legs. Eagles and falcons supported the arms. Angels soared across the chair's back accompanying a burning tree whose flames jutted above the top. The eyes of every angel and beast sparkled with inlaid garnets. The flames of the tree sparkled with amber and crimson rubies. The chair sat in the center of a dais on the bottom of the hexagonal tower built on a motte in the center of his fortress. Moat and forest and fields encircled the stronghold; David's kingdom stretched beyond the horizon in every direction.

David tapped his fingers on the armrests. His youthful beauty was a memory locked behind a protruding stomach and soft muscles. He was waiting for Nathanael the Wise in the chair from which he heard counsel, and judged.

Years ago, when he was young and honest, he relished these meetings. Now, Nathanael bore only accusations. From outside the tower, guards pushed open the double doors. Nathanael marched to King David without bowing or pausing. His staff clicked on the stone floor.

"May the Lord of the eternal fire that burns but does not consume bless you and shower mercy on your soul."

"And may he bless you likewise," David answered; his sigh rattled through the halls inspiring smirks from all quarters. "Your messenger said you had a vision, most urgent."

"I did. But I am not the only one. I met with Absalom before the sun rose to talk of ghosts, the ghost of Uriah."

"Absalom? Uriah's ghost?"

"Perhaps the dead hate treachery."

The two men glared at one another, an old bear and an old wolverine in a standoff. David raised his white knuckled fists as if he could hide his animosity and fear. Finally, as if he could dictate to the prophet of God, he motioned for Nathanael to continue.

"I heard a story the other day. I suspect the plaintiffs will come before you within a fortnight. A wealthy farmer pastures his flock of thirty ewes beside the fields of a poor farmer who owns but one. The poor man's ewe is marvelous, with long strands of wool and a shiny coat. The rich farmer covets her and when the poor farmer takes his grain to market, the rich farmer grabs the prized ewe from the poor man's barn."

"The rich man's entire herd should be given to the poor man," said David.

Nathanael nodded.

"An abomination. And if the rich man orders the poor man murdered on his way home to guarantee the ruse?"

"Why are you telling me this story?"

"Don't you know?"

David admired the way that Nathanael paused to acknowledge the silence that gripped the hall, even as his fingernails dug into his chair. David knew Nathanael's next words and yet the pause allowed him to hope.

"You are the rich man. You've disgraced yourself," said Nathanael. "Turned an honest wife into a harlot. Prayed for snow to cover your thieving trail. Conspired to slay your servant. It is beyond belief that one with so much can go to such extremes to take so little."

David stared at Nathanael's feet. The man wore no boots. He heard Nathanael's explanation long ago.

The Lord has not given me boots, therefore I do not need them.

"Did God tell you all this?"

"It pained Him to reveal so much wickedness; you are still a favored servant."

David covered his face in his hands and bowed his head, waiting.

"What more?"

"Nothing."

David dropped his hands from his face. Sunlight shot through the the six high narrow windows and fell on Nathanael's cheek.

The old man did not blink.

"Many will suffer," said David, "because of my rashness."

"If you do not tend the fire in your own house, other houses burn."

King David massaged his temples, another headache coming on like a storm brewing over the sea, where the clouds gather and billow and darken. There is nothing to do but watch and wait.

"Is there no penance?"

"No."

"And what of Uriah's ghost?"

"The ghost appeared near the gate and asked to speak with Absalom. He doesn't know what it wants."

"Is this ghost a harbinger of my sorrows?"

"Perhaps. The Lord does not explain His methods."

DAVID AWOKE TO A WET cloth pressed to his forehead. His angel hovered above him. Bathsheba. So beautiful. Her braided hair hung over her shoulder. If only she were a dream that would burn up like fog in the morning sun, something to be consumed at night with no consequence through the day. Bathsheba was the most potent of wines. A sip brought eternal craving and indulgence an eternal hangover.

She giggled when her almond eyes met his. She caused more jealousy among his wives than any other and why should she not? He could not give her up, nor did he wish to. He touched her cheek and she held his hand in place.

"I see you are feeling better," she said.

"An angel's touch may heal even the most grievous wounds." His fingertips trailed down her neck, across her breasts to the source of his troubles.

Bathsheba pressed his hand to her belly. "Do you feel him moving? It is a son. I can feel it. He kicks with the authority of a king."

"I doubt you not. It will be a son." David smiled at her, but his fingers trembled as they sometimes did on the eve of battle, when the killer angels gathered, and premonitions harassed him. *Sorrows will harass you.* "What's wrong?" she asked.

"Nothing." He raised himself and kissed her lips.

"Has Nathanael said anything about our child's future?"

"No," said David, too quickly. "And you mustn't ask him. The old man doesn't like to be pestered, especially by pretty girls."

Bathsheba laughed as she nuzzled David's chest.

"There is something you need to know. A rumor is spreading that Absalom spoke to Uriah's ghost."

"Is it true? Surely just a bit of gossip."

"Nathanael believes him."

"But why would he appear to Absalom?"

"A drunken man's delusions."

They kissed again.

Outside the curtained doorway, a woman cleared her throat.

"What?" shouted David.

Maachah parted the curtain and entered followed by Michal the Barren.

"Bathsheba is needed. Michal will attend you now," said Maachah.

"Needed?" said David. "She's pregnant. She should be resting."

"Embroidery is hardly laborious," said Maachah, "and we must all work to complete the new tapestries celebrating your victories."

David fell back on the pillows, waved his hand at Bathsheba, dismissing her. She left with a bewitching smile, mixing innocence and lust.

Michal sat on the edge of David's bed. David looked away. She whispered in his ear. "Should I tell the gossips why I am barren?"

"You wouldn't dare."

"I've heard that Uriah's ghost is walking the bailey. How many have seen him now?"

"Three I believe, but I suspect it's only rumors."

"Indeed. You are lucky only dead husbands come back to make trouble."

"You are referring to that sniveling weakling."

"He treated me as a wife, and never had I need to save his life."

"He did nothing. And he was never your husband."

ABSALOM WAITED OUTSIDE the great longhouse watching the autumn sun fall behind the forest. The fingers of his left hand curled around a leather collar that restrained the hound who sat on his haunches. As David's retainers entered the longhouse, they dipped their heads to Absalom in respect; kept a wary eye on the dog. Each man wore a necklace of gold and silver to honor their service. Joab the general was among them.

"Joab," said Absalom. "A word."

Joab nodded, his sunken eyes appraised and rejected Absalom's authority. "As you wish," he said as if in jest. Absalom motioned for Joab to follow. Despite his age, he stood tall. Even limping, he moved with the confidence of a much younger man. The two men and dog sauntered to the rear of the longhouse. Laughter and boasting echoed through the wattle.

"What happened to Uriah?"

"He died fighting before the gate of a Frisian fort. You could have asked this of anyone. That is no secret."

"Why was he engaged where the battle was most heated?"

"A brave warrior hears the battle and runs to it, as a snake pursues a mouse."

"I've heard you ordered him to lead the assault."

"He was brave. Warriors of his kind pursue the enemy," Joab said. "They don't hide behind a beast."

"You walk a treacherous line, Joab. You won't always be a favorite."

Absalom glared at the older man. Joab didn't blink or look away. Nor did he say more.

Absalom watched the old warrior limp away. Scars layered his arms and legs, one atop another like branches stacked for a fire. Someday, he thought. Someday that man will call me master.

AMNON WATCHED HER FROM the king's table, watched Tamar pouring mead into cups of wood or gourds—whatever would hold drink. She followed her mother Maachah, who offered wine to the retainers and their women. A silver circlet bound Tamar's auburn hair, which cascaded over her shoulders and past her waist. A girdle of leather and gold rings cinched her apron-skirt tight across her hips and breasts.

The men stole glances at her as she passed. Amnon knew he was not righteous, to lust after a half-sister, but he did lust. When she came near, he covered her hand with his. Her green eyes met his and then averted. He knew she was blushing, even as shadows whelmed her face.

As the eldest son, Amnon sat next to the King on the crowded bench. Amnon favored his left hand and frequently jostled David for space. Bathsheba, the pregnant new wife, the usurper, sat on the other side of David. They shared a joke and sipped their wine.

Tamar crowded next to Maachah at the end of the table. His half-sister didn't look at him. The way in which she didn't glance at him confirmed her feelings.

"Amnon," shouted David. "Have you seen Absalom?"

"Outside. With his damnable beast. Hunting ghosts I suspect."

David paused as if to ask more, but then Bathsheba said something funny and the pair laughed. They barely noticed the three musicians that gathered at the hearth, carrying a lyre, pan-pipes and a tambourine as wide as a man's chest. Three times the bard struck the rawhide stretched across the tambourine's frame. The thumps and jangle chased talk and laughter to the darkest recesses of the longhouse.

"The lay of our people," the bard announced with a practiced, sweeping flourish. "We humbly offer to our Lord on high and our king on earth."

The minstrels bowed and waited for David's assent.

"Sing," said David. "Sing to the Lord and His people, for it pleases Him."

The bard began slow and lugubrious. He sang of the great migration, the wandering through the black forest. He sang of the godly flame that burned without smoke, leaping from tree to tree, burning without consuming, crackling and roaring.

Amnon turned to Tamar, who watched the musicians with dull eyes and lips that neither smiled nor frowned. He leaned close to his father's ear. "Father, I'm not feeling well."

"What pains you? Your head?"

"And my stomach."

"Take some wine."

"I will. And send Tamar to me. Her singing will soothe my ills."

"Of course," said David.

Amnon walked behind the king's table and behind the tables. Tamar didn't acknowledge his passing, but that didn't concern him. She would not ignore her father's command.

ABSALOM WALKED AROUND the palisade's perimeter, diligent and wary and desperate for the ghost. He needed guidance and the ghost had told him things bright and preternatural. The hound ran beside him, and when Absalom stopped to search the shadowy spirals along the wall, the dog sat on his haunches—its snout pointing at the gibbous moon. Clamor and music spilled from the great longhouse. The bard would sing the "Lay of the Long Journey" and possibly another.

No mists swirled. Nothing groaned. Crickets chirped without pause. Absalom plodded on through dirt and grass. The hound loped alongside him.

If the ghost spoke truth and the living rumors were not idle, blood of treachery stained his father's hands. Such a man could not rule with trust and honor.

From the opposite side of the bailey, a sobbing wail brought Absalom and his hound to a stop. A lament sliced through the night, The dog stiffened. A woman's wails defied mending. Another ghost, he thought, another spirit to beguile.

Absalom saw her as she ran around the edge of a longhouse, and hesitated. The brooches were missing and her tattered shift slipped from her chest. A single brooch held at her right shoulder.

"Tamar," shouted Absalom. The girdle that had bound her waist was gone. Bruises striped her naked arm and shoulder. Tamar threw herself into Absalom's embrace, sobbing his name. He wrapped his bear-skin cape around her shoulders and held her until her sobs subsided.

"Who did this?"

New sobs drowned her speech.

"Tamar," he said.

"Amnon. He feigned sickness. Asked for wine. Father sent me."

From father to son, he thought, *spreading its poison through the branches. Greed and lust.* The ghost's words thumped his head, like an army beating their shields with swords.

"It was a trap," he said.

Tamar shook her head.

"Amnon is nothing to you. Come." He led her to his house, tugging her arm, as he walked. He bid her to rest while he secured his sword belt and hefted a bearded ax.

"I'll leave the hound outside."

"Don't kill him," she said.

"I'm not going to Amnon."

ABSALOM CARRIED HIS ax into the hall with the blade raised above his head. He strode between the tables and benches and loyal followers. He looked to neither side. The light from the hearth's flames danced in the rafters. The firelight glistened off the polished steel blade. Heads were lolling on the tables beside toppled cups; few remarked him. The bard was singing the lay of Goliath. He stood in Absalom's path, turned to him in mid-phrase; still singing as his voice trailed behind his senses. Absalom plowed past him, knocking him aside. The dropped tambourine jangled discordantly.

King David, drunk with mead and Bathsheba, slammed his fist into the table. "Absalom!"

A hush spread over the hall, a blanket of bewildered shock. Only the snapping fire and retainers lost to drunken snoring refused silence. No one moved.

Absalom covered the distance in three quick strides, mounted the dais, and buried his ax in the oaken table. Bathsheba screamed.

"Tamar," he said and then stopped to breathe, like a messenger who has run for miles. The weight of the words fell out in gasps and sobs. "Tamar has been raped."

"No," cried Maachah. "No. Tamar. Where? Where is she?"

Absalom eyed David.

"Who has done this," said David. "Let him hang from a tree until the crows have picked his bones."

The sycophants banged their cups in support. Michal knelt beside Maachah, folding her in a comforting embrace.

"Amnon," said Absalom. "Your son bears the guilt."

Anger drained from David's face. The chorus of cups ceased. Maachah wailed unabated. Michal hid her smirk.

"You bring us bad tidings, Absalom. We must have proof. Who told you? Who are the witnesses?"

"I have Tamar's word. Her bruises and torn clothing speak for themselves. No one else. Do you think Amnon would violate his sister in the courtyard?"

"Joab." David's gaze never strayed from Absalom. "Fetch Amnon to the tower. You'll find him in his house."

The old warrior motioned two soldiers to join him and marched away.

"Maachah and Michal," said David. "Go see to Tamar. Where is the girl?"

"She's resting in my house. I'll have to call off the hound. He's watching the door."

"Then do so," said David. "And bring her to the tower."

KING DAVID SAT IN THE oaken throne of the eternal fire, from where he dispensed judgments. Because the Lord favored his reign, he assumed his verdicts just and pleasing, but about this business his thoughts stumbled as a sailor lost in a rising tide on the verge of collapse, ready to suck all below.

The first blush of a red dawn lit the narrow eastern windows. A weak shaft of light crept among the shadows of the ceiling joists.

Amnon stood before the King. Maachah and Absalom flanked Tamar, who wore a black veil and Absalom's cloak.

Amnon stared at his father. Tamar bent her head toward the floor. Joab lurked at the edge of the shadows.

"What say you?" said David to Amnon. "Does Tamar lie?"

"She was not as I expected to find her," said Amnon, as if a buyer at a market

Tamar whimpered. Absalom held his sister to his chest.

"You have shielded your intentions from us, Amnon. Did you violate her?"

"A broken gate cannot be violated."

"Nor can it be shown when it was broken," said David.

Amnon said nothing.

"Where is Nathanael?" said Absalom.

"I am king and father," snapped David. "I don't need a prophet to pass judgment on my own children." *Infinite mercy is the domain of the infinitely good.* Those were Nathanael's words.

"The Lord loves all his children," said David. "Disciplines and forgiveness.... His greatness derives from mercy, not wrath." His family stared at him. David paused to gather his thoughts, for the road was uncharted and overgrown with thorns.

"I have suffered the sting of His anger," said David, "and savored the sweetness of His grace. No one knows the depths of His patience. Amnon, if she will have you, you shall marry Tamar and you shall praise her honor to all who will listen."

"No," shouted Absalom.

"I have judged and he will abide. A wise judge seeks healing *and* punishment, for the past *and* future."

"If the King won't defend his daughter, I will."

"It is done, Absalom," said Tamar.

"And if the holmgang speaks in my favor?" Absalom asked.

"Absalom, you confound me." David stood, his face crimson. "The matter is settled. The king's word is final."

"It is my challenge," said Absalom. "My right and duty."

David pressed his throbbing head between his palms. Cords of blood law tied his hands. "The judgment," he said, "will honor the outcome."

"We'll spread the hide tomorrow," said Absalom. Absalom ushered his sister and mother out the door.

"Joab," said David. "Take Amnon to his house and keep him there until the holmgang."

"Am I a prisoner?"

"I should have you executed. If not...." David held his tongue. "Leave me."

"If not what, father? Tell me what stayed your hand."

"The Lord's mercy stayed my hand. Leave me, I said."

Joab led David's son away. The King held his aching head as the dawn greeted the walls with rouge.

JOAB STOOD INSIDE THE door of Amnon's house.

"Absalom will kill you."

"Let him try."

"You are not afraid?"

"Is there purpose in your warning or idle rambling?"

Joab stared hard at Amnon as he scratched his beard. "Absalom has become a nuisance. A house can't tolerate wayward timber."

"Many speak ill of my father, the King."

"Absalom may do more than talk."

"And he doesn't like you very much, does he?"

"I serve David's interests."

"You want me to kill him. But I'll have to kill him anyway to save my own life. This is your doing, isn't it?"

"A victor strikes an enemy before he's ready. Your father doesn't have the heart."

"What's your plan?"

"I can smear a poison on the blade of your ax. A nick will kill him."

"And you will protect me."

"Who will avenge him? He's asking for a combat to the death."

"Rightly so," said Amnon. "And you're an old fool. If Absalom falls dead from a scratch, the King will note it. Everyone will know I poisoned him. I'll hang, but you'll get what you want. Very clever, Joab."

"I misjudged you."

"You're vulnerable now, Joab. I'll remember this."

Joab turned to the door and then stopped. "Why is it you will not take Tamar? Even an old man can see her charms."

"I only wanted a taste and she was bitter. The sight of her burns my eyes."

DAVID SAT IN THE OAKEN throne, listening to Joab. With every word, he felt his head. Something wicked was growing inside his house, inside his kingdom.

"He stands outside the gate with his dog," said Joab. "I've seen him myself."

David sighed. "Go on."

"He stands before the gate and stops everyone. 'There is no king on the throne,' he tells them. 'There is no just man there to hear your pleas.' It is treason."

"It is an angry young man. He does not know the world. Mayhap he has truly spoken to Uriah's ghost."

"You must punish Absalom, publicly. His transgressions cannot be ignored."

"If his mind is addled, the holmgang will sober him. I've been thinking to honor Uriah."

As David spoke, one of the double doors swung open. Uzzah stepped past Joab and dropped to one knee.

"Forgive me, my king, but I bear wretched tidings. It is Bathsheba."

David leapt to his feet.

"What? What? What has happened?"

"Absalom," said Joab. "Coming to claim your wives."

"He'll suffer the cold steel if he's laid a hand on her."

"No, no," said Uzzah. "She has miscarried."

Sorrows will harass you, bring your kingdom to the point of breaking.

"It is the Lord's doing," he said. He stared past Joab and Uzzah with glassy, vacant eyes. "In the course of a day, I have lost three sons and one will never come home."

The King walked between Uzzah and Joab. The doors opened when he shouted a command. He left the confines of the tower for the bright sunshine of the gate. Joab and Uzzah followed. David stopped before one of the fire pits where he could see Absalom standing with his hound, accosting all who passed. David knelt, scooped charred wood and gray ashes into his cupped hands. Ash sifted through his fingers, forming a gray cloud in the breeze. David, the King, raised his hands and poured sorrow over his head.

ABSALOM COULD NOT SLEEP. Tamar rested in his bed, curled atop an elk hide blanket. Their mother sat with her, stroking Tamar's auburn hair, as she had done years ago.

"What if I am with child?" Tamar asked. "It will have no father."

Maachah looked to Absalom. Words failed her.

"Father has lost his mind. A union with Amnon? Would be an abomination."

He left Maachah and Tamar and walked the palisade's perimeter with his hound, as he had done the night before.

"Uriah," he shouted.

The guards on the wall stared down at him. Some shared his doubts. Others found his shouts more frightening than any ghost. The guards talked of the coming holmgang. Had Joab's warriors not guarded Amnon's house, he would have hastened there to snap his brother's neck and cast the body into a food trough for crows and dogs.

Absalom neared the turning where the ghost had first appeared, his footfalls thudding in the trampled dirt; the dog padded beside him. The moon lighted a path darkened by shadows.

"Uriah," he cried. "Have you no more honor than the King?"

The hound stiffened and growled. Absalom scanned the darkness.

"Uriah?"

"Absalom." The voice was a woman's, soft and soothing.

Absalom furrowed his brows. "Who's there?"

Michal stepped from the shadows. Her face glowed white in the moonlight, framed by her black hair. Her lapis-blue shift seemed to float.

"Michal?"

"Call back your dog," she said.

He told the hound to sit, but it ignored him. Absalom pushed down on its back, settling the hound on its haunches. It snarled at the darkest point of the turning, at solid darkness.

"You are seeking a ghost," she said.

"The spirit knows the future," said Absalom.

Michal stepped closer, her scented oils wrapping him in a sweet cocoon. "I seek the future as well, but I am searching for the new king."

"The new king?"

"In the land of the living. David no longer rules. He clings to power like an oak holds its dead leaves. A wind is coming, Absalom. Does David defend his daughter? His servants?"

"No."

"Someone must be that wind that tears the power from his hands. What will you do?"

"King David has many friends."

"Do you know why I am barren? He fears a grandchild of Saul will challenge his legitimacy, so he locks me in an empty bed, wasting away with my passions."

"That is indeed cruel."

"And cowardly. Take the king's wife, Absalom. Lay with me."

He lifted her and kissed her and took her near the wall where they tumbled into the shadows, a jumble of arms, legs, and clothing. Michal made no effort to hide her joy and the guards heard.

The hound growled at the dark turning, giving no attention to the lovers. Laughter, faint and far, echoed in the shadows. A gust of wind whipped dead leaves into a spiral. Then they were gone, the laughter and the wind; only the hound had heard them.

BENEATH THE TOWER, holmgangs began at midday, when the sun would not favor either man. Short stakes secured the corners of an ox hide. Four hazel staves marked the outer boundary, the line of forfeiture.

David sat below the tower doors. A fresh layer of ash dulled his black hair's luster.

Men, women, and children crowded around the three remaining sides. Some sat on the walkway that edged the palisade, their legs dangling over the side. Everyone who could come came. One of the fighters might be king some day and the other would die bleeding on ox hide. All affirmed the holmgang's sacred truth.

Absalom held his war ax. Three wooden shields with iron bands had been arranged just outside the line of forfeiture.

"Where's Tamar?" Absalom asked his mother.

"Resting," said Maachah. "She wouldn't come. Said she couldn't watch you die."

"I'm not the one dying." Absalom looked across the hide. Amnon stood with war ax and three shields. "The Lord will punish the wicked, mother. I have faith in His justice."

Amnon's mother whispered in her son's ear. Michal stood behind her and smiled when her eyes met Absalom's. Absalom turned to his shields, ordered and equidistant. Until last night he was beyond reproach. The ghost said *there is a festering sore at the heart of your house, spreading its poison through the branches*. He was a branch as surely as Amnon.

The hound barked and lurched toward the hide. Absalom slapped Uzzah. "Hold him firm I told you."

Uzzah's face reddened as he tugged the hound back to a sitting position.

"Yes," he said through clenched teeth. The strain compressed his voice to a whisper.

David rose and stepped forward onto the hide. He looked from Absalom to Amnon. "It is custom that demands I ask you if your differences cannot be resolved without combat."

They shook their heads.

"And a father's love demands I ask again."

Silence greeted David.

"So be it. I vest Joab the authority to judge. May the Lord guide the righteous weapon and spare the guilty death. Absalom, your terms."

Absalom answered without hesitation. "Until death or forfeiture."

A hush rippled through the crowd.

"I expected as much. Joab, their contest is yours."

David eyed each young man before making his way back to his bench. Does he know about Michal, wondered Absalom. David usually knows all, but who would tell him and who would believe her story?

"Arm yourselves," said Joab.

Absalom donned a helm with a chainmail curtain. He fitted a round shield to his forearm and took up his battle ax. Across the hide, Amnon did the same, but held his ax in his left hand.

At a signal, they crossed the boundary, stepped to the hide, and thumped shields. They leapt back as the shields clacked to give the impact a hollow sound. As the challenged, Amnon had the right of first strike. Amnon charged. Absalom blocked. Amnon attacked with a flurry of swings; each stroke drove his brother back. Absalom had little experience against a left-handed foe. He twisted out of position to block Amnon. As he neared the line of forfeiture, Absalom lunged forward, swinging low. He sliced Amnon's thigh. Amnon retreated. Blood stained his leggings and dripped down to his boots.

They moved about the hide exchanging blows. Uzzah exercised all his strength to hold the hound, who rallied whenever Amnon swung. David watched the contest. He didn't twitch or lean forward. Only when someone stepped near the line of forfeiture did he look to Joab for a signal but none came.

When Absalom's shield splintered into three pieces, Joab called a halt.

Absalom and Amnon gulped water from gourds, as they fitted new shields to their forearms.

"Have you had enough, brother?" shouted Amnon.

Absalom eyed his foe for only a moment.

"Surely we have seen enough," said David.

The King's suggestion startled the crowd and set them to murmuring.

"The terms cannot be altered," said Joab. "You know that well. It is the ancient way."

"The Ancient Days did not make laws for us to fall upon as a vanquished captain falls on his sword." David studied the faces of his people. Implacable, they stared back as one, branches from a single bole waiting for affirmation. Where was Nathanael? Walking in the woods, no doubt. He should have consulted Nathanael. David brushed ash from his cheeks.

"Let it continue," he said.

Joab looked square at Uzzah and nodded. Absalom and Amnon stepped onto the hide. Joab raised his right hand, and when he swung it down, their shields clacked together. The crowd hushed as the pair attacked with new ferocity, driving one another over the hide. Thuds and grunts punctuated the fight.

Amnon landed a blow square on Absalom's shield. The shield deflected none of the hit's force and Absalom suffered its full weight and shivered. He stumbled, catching his heel on one of the short stakes. He fell backward as his legs shot forward. He fought the instinct to spread his arms for balance, keeping his shield in front of his chest. Wind burst from his lungs. When he struck the earth, his helm bounced from his head.

David turned away. Maachah screamed. Amnon raised his ax high, ready. Uzzah let go. The hound leapt, crashing into Amnon as he swung. The ax wheeled through the air. Amnon toppled. The hound lunged for Amnon's throat, but Amnon struck first with his shield, knocking the beast away. It yelped as it rolled. Amnon sank his ax into its chest. The hound's dark eyes rolled backward.

If he had time to think, Amnon would have relished killing the beast, so much did he hate it. He sat up on his knees, looking down at the dog, his ax dripping blood, his arm tensed to strike again. The crowd booed. Some shouted foul.

Absalom's dog.

Absalom.

As Amnon scrambled to stand, he caught a glimpse of his mother, her face crinkled in an anguished scream. Why should she scream, he thought. The beast is dead and Absalom has fallen. One more killing blow to mix the blood of master and servant, he thought as Absalom's blade cleaved his helm and wedged deep into bone and brain. Absalom could not remove it. He let loose of the handle. Blood rained down Amnon's face, his puzzled eyes on his mother. Amnon's body fell across the hound. The handle of Absalom's ax pointed to the tower.

Absalom looked to Joab. The old warrior nodded. He looked to the King, who stood at the edge of the hide. The King moved his mouth but no words came. He breathed deeply and tried again.

"The holmgang has spoken," he said.

Angry shouts rose from Amnon's supporters.

Joab held up his hand and the people fell still.

"The Lord has spoken," said David. "He has meted out his justice. Let this be an end to it."

DAVID SAT ON THE THRONE of the eternal fire. His elbows rested on his knees. Hunched forward he no longer filled the throne. His tunic hung loose and torn from his chest. Ash stained his face and arms, his leggings and boots.

Absalom faced his father, his clothes intact and free of ash. Amnon's body lay between them.

"Has justice been done?" said David.

"Holmgang has spoken the Lord's will."

"Did we truly hear what was said?"

"The crime has been punished. Something you wouldn't do."

"When I was young I saw justice as a staff, stiff and certain to lean on. Now it is like smoke. I see it and smell it and feel it. I know what it is, but I cannot hold it. We are fallible, Absalom. Fallen. We shoot our arrows through the mists as we face the sunrise."

"You've strayed from the path into the bog. That's what Nathanael will tell you."

"Do you speak for prophets now?"

Absalom did not answer.

"And how will you punish your own crime when you are king?"

"My crime?"

"Did you think you could fornicate with Michal in the bailey in private? Your ancient path ends in a tree, Absalom."

"Michal tells me she is wife in name only, that the King neglects her. Do you care so much for your castoff?"

"I thought you adhered to the law. Michal is a dangerous woman. She metes out great love and equal hatred. I've felt both. She betrayed her father once. She has betrayed me, and she will betray you."

"I've given her no cause."

David sighed. The Frisians surrendered land with far less effort. "To punish as the Lord is easy, but to show his mercy requires discipline and wisdom. A great king can emulate his master with both hands. Weakness, Absalom, favors only one."

"The ghost spoke of *a festering sore at the heart of your house.* I rebuked him, but I see now that he spoke the truth."

"Was it Uriah?"

"Maybe. It spoke true."

"And what did this ghost predict?"

"Tamar's troubles."

"And?"

"The ghost hasn't shown itself again."

"You should not seek counsel from the dead; certainly not the vengeful dead."

"I find the dead more honest."

"You should fear the one with nothing to lose."

"He wants vengeance on you, father. Not me."

"You seek counsel from a ghost who desires my ruin," said David.

Shouting outside the tower doors ended their talk. The doors burst open. Joab entered carrying Tamar's body. Her auburn hair, dark and wet, hung past his knees. A garland of flowers—white and red and purple—encircled her neck. Maachah followed, clinging to Michal. Water darkened their skirts.

"We found her beneath the ancient willow," said Michal, "submerged in the brook."

Absalom rushed at Joab and snatched his sister's body. Joab released his burden without a struggle.

"No." David stood, his cry echoing off the stone walls. "No, no, no." His voice trailed off as he collapsed, hid his face in his hands, and wept. *Many will suffer. Those eyes might cost a thousand lives.* Absalom laid Tamar's body at the foot of the throne. No one spoke.

"You sniveling old man," said Absalom. "What have you done? Speak it, so your days as king may end."

"Do not speak treason, Absalom." Joab drew his sword.

"Do you serve the people or an old man?"

"A king serves and leads his people. I am King David's hound."

Absalom looked at his father, at the ash-stained head with a bald spot spreading from its crown. "You are finished," he said.

He dashed past his mother and Michal; out the open tower doors.

"Joab," said David. "Fetch him back. Bring my son back to me."

JOAB CREPT ALONG A path in the woods; an ash spear doubled as his walking stick. As he neared the brook, he heard cursing, Absalom's cursing. He stepped from behind a blackberry bramble. The brook slowed and widened near an ancient willow that Joab knew well. As a boy, Joab had climbed this tree and dreamed of warfare.

Inside the weeping leaves, Absalom cursed his father and lamented his dead sister. Joab almost pitied the boy. Absalom and men of his ilk were soft, easily trapped. Joab's boots splashed only twice as he crossed the brook and stopped at the willow's shade. Absalom's back rested against a branch. His leg twisted where his foot had lodged in the crook of two branches. Absalom laughed as he saw the old warrior.

"Joab, an old man has sent another old man to fetch me."

"That was the King's wish."

"The King." Absalom laughed. "You'll do whatever he asks."

"I loyally serve."

"And if there is a new king?"

"It will depend upon his worth. A king demands service. He does not beg for it."

"Then get me out of this tree."

Joab hefted his spear. Absalom had only a second to lose his smirk, which shrank to fear.

DAVID PERCHED ON THE edge of his throne. Carved flames of orange and red amber and rubies normally shielded from view shone behind him. Three shrouded bodies lay on the floor. Dark red stains bloomed over the white linen. Narrow shafts of light filtered through the west windows and crawled high on the eastern walls.

Nathanael and Joab stood in the hall.

"He resisted," said Joab.

"You have been steadfastly loyal to me, Joab. But this...." He gestured at the bodies. "Have we come to the end?"

The old prophet shook his head.

"Your sighs will harry you; every night you will drench your bed with tears."

BLOOD AND BEAUTY AND OTHER WEIRD TALES

Dear Readers,

Thank you so much for reading the stories in *Blood and Beauty and Other Weird Tales*. There's a lot of variation in these tales, ranging from steampunk to fantasy to horror. Story collections are usually a grab bag so I hope you found some that you enjoyed.

I would love to hear what you thought of these stories. You can contact me directly through my website or you can leave a review on Goodreads[1] or wherever you downloaded this book. Believe me, writers are starved for feedback.

If this is your first taste of my writing, there's plenty more. You can find a list of my books on my website. Better yet, you can sign up for my Readers Group and receive two short stories (**"The Ivy and the Walnut"** and **"The Wand"**) exclusive to Readers Group members.

To leave feedback, find my books, or join my Readers Group, visit my website at jeffchapmanbooks.com[2].

Thanks for reading and have a great day,
Jeff

---

1. http://www.goodreads.com/book/show/25511136-blood-and-beauty-and-other-weird-tales

2. http://jeffchapmanbooks.com/

About the Author

Jeff Chapman writes software by day and speculative fiction when he should be sleeping. His tales range from fantasy to horror, and they don't all end badly. He lives with his wife, children, and cats in a house with more books than bookshelf space.

You can find me on my Goodreads Author Page[1], on Facebook[2], or check out my musings on words and fiction at jeffchapmanbooks.com[3].

WANT A COUPLE FREE ebooks? Want to stay up to date on new titles and special offers?

Consider subscribing to my Very Important Readers Group[4]. My short stories **"The Ivy and the Walnut"** and **"The Wand"** are *only* available to readers in my Readers Group.

Go here to get started: jeffchapmanbooks.com[5].

---

1. http://www.goodreads.com/JeffChapman

2. http://www.facebook.com/JeffChapmanWriter

3. http://jeffchapmanbooks.com

4. http://jeffchapmanbooks.com/

5. http://jeffchapmanbooks.com/

Publication History

"BLOOD AND BEAUTY" originally appeared in Songs of the Satyrs, 2014 and 2015. Copyright © Jeff Chapman, 2014.

"Sutter's Well" originally appeared in *Plasma Frequency Magazine*, Issue 9, December/January 2013/14. Copyright © Jeff Chapman, 2013.

"Morphine and Chocolate" originally appeared in *Midnight Diner 4: Wastelands Under the Sun*, 2013. Copyright © Jeff Chapman, 2013.

"The Facts in the Case of M. Hussman" originally appeared in *Bards and Sages Quarterly*, July 2013. Copyright © Jeff Chapman, 2013.

"Shafts to Hell" originally appeared in *How the West Was Wicked*, 2011. Copyright © Jeff Chapman, 2011.

"Good King David" originally appeared in *King David and the Spiders from Mars*, 2014. Copyright © Jeff Chapman, 2014.

Don't miss out!

Visit the website below and you can sign up to receive emails whenever Jeff Chapman publishes a new book. There's no charge and no obligation.

https://books2read.com/r/B-A-YLKF-ENLLB

BOOKS 2 READ

Connecting independent readers to independent writers.

Also by Jeff Chapman

Comic Cat Tales
The Cat Lady Is Always Right
A Cat Called Blackjack

Huckster Tales
The Black Blade

The Cats of Incognito Lane
Chasing the Great Corvid: An Incognito Lane Tale

Standalone
Last Request: A Victorian Gothic
Blood and Beauty and Other Weird Tales
Strange Paths to Wonder: Fantasy Stories
Krampus Comes to Town

Watch for more at https://www.jeffchapmanbooks.com/.